A Night
for Murder—

The man walking on the sidewalk didn't even look up when the sedan squealed around the corner. He walked with nonchalant arrogance, this man, dressed in expensive good taste. The automobile squealed around the corner and headed directly for the curb. It pulled up about ten feet ahead of the walking man.

The muzzle of a rifle appeared at one of the windows. The man walking broke his stride for just an instant. There was a sudden blurring flash of yellow and a shockingly loud explosion. . . .

Sy Kramer had received a *Killer's Payoff.*

Killer's Payoff

An 87th Precinct Mystery

by Ed McBain

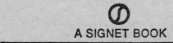

A SIGNET BOOK

NEW AMERICAN LIBRARY

The city in these pages is imaginary.
The people, the places are all fictitious.
Only the police routine is based on established
investigatory technique.

SIGNET TRADEMARK REG. U.S. PAT. OFF. AND FOREIGN COUNTRIES
REGISTERED TRADEMARK—MARCA REGISTRADA
HECHO EN CHICAGO, U.S.A.

SIGNET, SIGNET CLASSIC, MENTOR, ONYX, PLUME, MERIDIAN AND
NAL BOOKS *are published by NAL PENGUIN INC.,*
1633 Broadway, New York, New York 10019

FIRST PRINTING, JUNE, 1974

6 7 8 9 10 11 12 13 14

PRINTED IN THE UNITED STATES OF AMERICA

Chapter 1

It could have been 1937.

It might have looked like this on a night in late June, the sidewalks washed with a light drizzle, the asphalt glistening slickly, blackly, in the splash of red and green neons. Despite the drizzle, there would be a balmy touch to the air, the fragrant smell of June, the delicate aroma of bursting greenery. And the perfume of growing things would mingle with the perfume of passing women, mingle with the perfume of people and machines, mingle with the ever-present smell of the city at night.

The clothes would have looked different, the women's skirts a little shorter, the men's coats sporting small black-velvet collars, perhaps. The automobiles would have been square and black. The shop windows would have carried the blue eagle of the National Recovery Act. There would have been small differences, but a city does not really change much over the years, because a city is only a collection of people and people are timeless. And the way the automobile came around the corner, it could have been 1937.

The man walking on the sidewalk didn't even look up when the sedan squealed around the corner. He was city-born and city-bred, and the sound of shrieking tires was not an alien sound to him. He walked with nonchalant arrogance, this man, dressed in expensive good taste. He walked with the sure knowledge that all was right with the world, the certainty that he was master of all he surveyed. The automobile squealed around the corner and headed directly for the curb. It pulled up about ten feet ahead of the walking man. The windows on the side facing the curb were open. The engine idled.

The muzzle of a rifle appeared at one of the windows. The man walking broke his stride for just an instant. The person about to fire the rifle was looking through a telescopic sight down the length of the barrel. The distance between the muzzle's end and the walking man was no more

5

than eight feet. There was a sudden blurring flash of yellow, and then a shockingly loud explosion. The man's face erupted in flying fragments; the rifle was pulled back from the window. There was a moment, and then the car gunned away from the curb, tires burning rubber, shrieking into the night. The man on the sidewalk lay bleeding profusely, and the drizzle softly covered him like a shroud.

It could have been 1937.

But it wasn't.

A pair of green globes straddled the entrance doorway to the precinct. For the benefit of those who might have missed one or another of the globes, the numerals 87 were lettered onto both in black paint. Seven gray stone steps led from the sidewalk to the entrance doorway. Just inside the doorway, the desk sergeant sat behind the high desk, looking like a defrocked magistrate. A sign on the desk warned all visitors that they must stop there before proceeding further. Just beyond the desk and opposite it, a rectangle of wood that had been shaped into a pointing hand and then painted white announced, DETECTIVE DIVISION. The pointing hand indicated a double flight of metal stairs that led to the second floor of the precinct building. The locker room was at one end of the corridor on the second floor. The detective squadroom was at the other end, separated from the corridor by a slatted rail divider. Between the locker room and the squadroom, there were two benches, the clerical office, the men's lavatory, and a room marked INTERROGATION.

The squadroom behind the slatted rail divider was sometimes called the "Bull Pen" by the uniformed cops of the precinct. The title was delivered with affectionate envy, for it was here that the detectives, the élite, the bulls of the 87th, conducted their business.

On the morning of June twenty-seventh, Detective Bert Kling's business was with a man named Mario Torr.

Torr had come to the station house of his own volition, had mounted the seven gray stone steps, stopped at the desk as requested, asked for the detectives, and been directed to the pointing hand opposite the desk. He had climbed to the second floor of the building, entered the dimly lighted corridor there, hesitated a moment, and then walked to the end of the corridor, where he'd waited outside the railing until one of the detectives had asked him what he wanted. Torr was dressed in ready-to-wear mediocrity. There are men who can make a thirty-five-dollar suit look as if it were handtailored. Torr was not one of these men. He wore his brown sharkskin as if it belonged to his fatter brother. His tie had been picked up in a three-for-a-dollar tie shop along The Stem. His white shirt had been laundered too often. The cuffs and collar were frayed.

There was, in fact, a frayed appearance to the entire man who was Mario Torr. He needed a haircut, and he had not shaved too closely that morning, and his teeth did not look very white or very clean. Worse, he looked as if he knew he was not dapper. He looked as if he had wilted and didn't know how the hell to unwilt.

He sat opposite Kling at one of the desks, and his eyes blinked nervously. He was apparently not too comfortable inside a police precinct, and even less comfortable talking to a detective in a squadroom. He spoke to Kling with the hesitant, distrustful sincerity of a disbeliever on a psychiatrist's couch for the first time. All the while, his eyes blinked and his hands picked imaginary lint from the too clean, spotlessly mediocre, brown sharkskin suit.

"You know his name was Sy Kramer, huh?" Torr asked.

"Yes," Kling said. "We got a positive identification from his fingerprints."

"Sure. I figured you already knew that."

"Besides, he was carrying a wallet with identification. And five hundred dollars in cash."

Torr nodded reflectively. "Yeah, he was a big spender, Sy was."

"He was a blackmailer," Kling said flatly.

"Oh, you know that, too, huh?"

"I told you we identified him from his prints, didn't I?"

"Mmm," Torr said. "Tell me something."

"What would you like to know?"

"You figure this for a gang kill?"

"It looks that way," Kling said.

"Does that mean you'll just let it drop?"

"Hell, no. Murder is murder."

"But you're starting with gang stuff, huh?"

"We've got a few feelers out," Kling said. "Why? Are you selling information, Torr? Is that why you're here?"

"Me?" Torr looked seriously offended. "Do I look like a stoolie?"

"I don't know what you look like. Why *are* you here?"

"Sy was a friend of mine."

"A close friend?"

"Well, we shot a game of pool together every now and then. Who'll be working on this case?"

"Detectives Carella and Hawes caught the squeal. It's their case. The rest of us'll help if we're needed. You still haven't told me why you're here, Torr."

"Well, I don't think this was a gang kill. The papers said a hunting rifle got him. Is that right?"

"According to Ballistics, it was a .300 Savage, yes."

"Does that sound like a gang kill? Listen, I asked around. Nobody had anything against Sy. There was no beef. How could there be? He was a loner. He never got involved with any of the racket boys. Blackmail you do alone. The more people who know, the more ways you've got to split."

"You seem to know a lot about it," Kling said.

"Well, I get around."

"Sure."

"So it's my idea that one of Sy's marks—you know, somebody he was giving the squeeze—decided it was time to get rid of him. That's my idea."

"Would you happen to know who his marks were?"

"No. But they must've been big. Sy always had plenty of money. A big spender he was, Sy." Torr paused. "Do you? Know who the marks were, I mean?"

"No," Kling said, "but of course we'll look into it. I still don't know why you're so interested, Torr."

"He was my friend," Torr said simply. "I want to see justice done."

"You can rest assured we'll do everything in our power," Kling said.

"Thanks," Torr said. "It's just cause he was my friend, you understand. And I think you're taking the wrong approach with this 'Gangland Murder' garbage the newspapers are printing."

"We have no control over the press, Mr. Torr," Kling said.

"Sure, but I wanted you to know what I thought. Cause he was my friend, Sy was."

"We'll look into it," Kling said. "Thanks for coming up."

The first thing Kling did when Torr left the squadroom was to call the Bureau of Criminal Identification.

The bureau was located at Headquarters, downtown on

High Street. It was open twenty-four hours a day, and its sole reason for existence was the collection, compilation, and cataloguing of any and all information descriptive of criminals. The I.B. maintained a Fingerprint File, a Crimi-

IDENTIFICATION BUREAU

Name__Mario Albert Torressa__

Identification Jacket Number__A 720471__

Alias__Mario Torr, Al Torr_____Color__White__

Residence__6312 North 11th, Isola__

Date of Birth____September 5, 1917_____Age__34__

Birthplace____Riverhead__

Height__5' 8"__Weight__147__Hair__Black__Eyes__Brown__

Complexion__Dark_____Occupation__Laborer__

Scars and Tattoos__Mastoid operation scars behind both ears.__

__Appendectomy scar on abdomen.__

Arrested by__Detective 1st/Grade Samuel Lipschitz__

Detective Division Number__12-637-1952__

Date of Arrest__1/19/52__Place__Breger Avenue, Isola__

Charge__Extortion__

Brief Details of Crime__Torr, having learned that a man was an__

__ex-convict gainfully employed but without employer's know-__

__ledge of prison record, called the man and demanded $5,000__

__lest he reveal knowledge to employer. The man notified the__

__police. Detective Lipschitz concealed himself in Breger__

__Avenue apartment, listened to Torr's extortion threats when__

__he arrived to claim payment, and made the arrest.__

Previous Record__Arrested for blackmail attempt in 1949. Re-__

__leased when witness withdrew.__

Indicted__Criminal Courts, January 20, 1952__

Final Charge__Extortion, Penal Law Sections 850, 851, Sub-__

__division Four of latter__

Disposition__One to two years at Castleview Prison, Jessamyn__

nal Index File, a Degenerate File, a Parolee File, a Released Prisoner File, a Known Gamblers, Known Rapists,
Known Burglars, Known Muggers, Known Any-and-All
Kinds of Criminal File. Its Modus Operandi File contained
more than 80,000 photographs of known criminals. And
since all persons charged with and convicted of a crime
were photographed and fingerprinted, as specified by law,
the file was continually growing and continually being
brought up to date. The I.B. received and classified some
206,000 sets of prints yearly, and it answered requests for
some 250,000 criminal records from police departments all
over the country. When Kling asked for whatever they had
on a man named Mario Torr, the I.B. dug into its files and
sent Kling the photostated tickets before noon.

Kling was not at all interested in the fingerprints that
were in the envelope. He scanned them rapidly, and then
picked up the copy of Mario Torr's sheet.

There was in the Penal Law a subtle distinction between
extortion and blackmail.

Section 850 defined extortion as "the obtaining of property from another, or the obtaining the property of a corpo-
ration from an officer, agent or employee thereof, with the
consent, induced by a wrongful use of force or fear, or under color of official right."

Section 851 picked up where 850 left off, with a defini-
tion of what threats may constitute extortion: "Fear, such
as will constitute extortion may be induced by an *oral* or
written threat: 1. To . . . ," etc., etc. The subdivision uti-
lized in the charge against Torr had been subdivision 4:
". . . oral or written threat: 4. To expose any secret affect-
ing him or any of them."

Such was the nature of extortion.

Blackmail was extortion in writing.

Section 856 of the Penal Law stated that "A person who
. . . causes to be forwarded or received . . . any letter or
writing, threatening: 1. To accuse . . . 2. To do any injury
. . . 3. To publish or connive at publishing any libel . . .
4. To expose . . . ," etc., is guilty of blackmail.

The distinction was indeed a subtle one in that blackmail
had to be in writing, whereas extortion could be either oral
or written. In any case, Torr was both a convicted extortionist and an accused blackmailer.

Kling shrugged and looked through the rest of the photostated material in the I.B.'s packet. Torr had served a

year at Castleview, the state's—and possibly the nation's—worst penitentiary. He had been released on parole at the end of that time, after receiving a guarantee of employment from a construction company out on Sand's Spit. He had in no way violated his parole. Nor had he been arrested again since his prison term had ended. He was, at present, still gainfully employed by the same Sand's Spit construction company, earning good wages as a laborer.

He seemed to be a decent, upright, honest citizen.

And yet he was interested in the apparent gangland murder of a known blackmailer.

And Bert Kling wondered why.

Chapter 2

There had been a time when Detective Steve Carella had considered Danny Gimp just another stool pigeon. He had considered him a good stoolie, true, and a valuable stoolie —but nonetheless a pigeon, a somewhat-pariah who roamed the nether world between criminal and law-enforcement officer. There had been a time when, had Danny Gimp dared to call Carella "Steve," the detective would have taken offense.

All that had been before December.

In December, Steve Carella had managed to get himself shot. He would never forgive himself for having been shot that day in December. In fact, he would always refer to December twenty-second as the day of his idiocy, and he would allow that idiotic day to live in his memory as a reminder never to rush in where angels feared. He truthfully had come very close to joining the band of angels on those few days before Christmas. Somehow, miraculously, he'd managed to survive.

And it was then that he had learned Danny Gimp was waiting downstairs to see him.

Steve Carella had been a very surprised cop. Danny Gimp entered the hospital room. He'd been wearing his good suit, and a clean shirt, and he'd carried a box of candy under his arm, and he'd embarrassedly handed Carella the gift and then mumbled, "I'm . . . I'm glad you made it, Steve." They had talked until the nurse had said it was time for Danny to go. Carella had taken his hand in a firm clasp, and it was then that Danny had ceased being just another stool pigeon and become a human being.

On the morning of June twenty-eighth, after a call from Carella, Danny limped into the squadroom of the 87th Precinct. The bulls on the squad had recently wrapped up the murder of a girl who'd worked in a liquor store, and now they were up to their ears in another homicide, and this one seemed to require the special talents of Danny Gimp. The men of the 87th would not be called for testimony in the trial of Marna Phelps until August—but this was June, and there was work to be done, and you didn't sit around on your ass waiting for trials if you wanted to earn your salary. If you wanted to earn your salary, you got up from behind your desk the moment you saw Danny standing at the slatted rail divider. You went to him with your hand extended, and you greeted him the way few policemen greet stool pigeons. But Danny Gimp was not a stool pigeon to you. Danny Gimp was a human being.

"Hello, Steve," Danny said. "Hot enough for you?"

"Not too bad," Carella said. "You're looking good. How've you been?"

"Fine, fine," Danny said. "The rain slaughtered my leg, but you know how that is. I'm glad it cleared up."

Danny Gimp had had polio as a child. The disease had not truly crippled him, although it had left him with the limp that would provide his lifelong nickname. Carella knew that old wounds ached when it rained. He had old wounds to prove it. It came as no surprise that Danny's leg had bothered him during the past week of rain. It would have come as a surprise to Carella to learn that Danny harbored no ill feeling toward his leg or the disease that had caused his limp. It would have come as a greater surprise to learn that Danny Gimp lighted a candle in church each week for a man named Jonas Salk.

The men walked into the squadroom. At a near-by desk, Cotton Hawes looked up from his typing. Bert Kling, closer to the grilled windows that fronted on Grover Park, was busy talking on the telephone. Carella sat, and Danny sat opposite him.

"So what can I sell you?" Danny asked, smiling.

"Sy Kramer," Carella said.

"Yeah," Danny answered, nodding.

"Anything?"

"A crumb," Danny said. "Blackmail, extortion, the works. Living high on the hog for the past nine months or so. He musta latched onto something good."

"Any idea what it was?"

"Nope. Want me to go on the earie?"

"I think so. What about this killing the other night?"

"Lots of scuttlebutt on it, Steve. A thing like that, you figure right away the racket boys. Not so, from what I can pick up."

"No, huh?"

"If it was, it's being kept mighty cool. This is old hat, any-way, this torpedo crap. Who hires guns nowadays? And if you do, you don't do it up dramatic, you dig me, Steve? This crap went out with movies about bootleg whisky. If you need somebody out of the way, you get him out of the way—but you don't come screaming around corners in black limousines with machine guns blazing. Once in a while you get something with flair. The rest of the time it's a quiet plop, not a noisy bang. You dig?"

"I dig," Carella said.

"And if this was a gang thing, I'd've heard about it. There ain't much I don't hear. If this was a gang thing, there'd be some jerk havin' a beer and spillin' over at the mouth. I figure it different."

"How do you figure it?"

"One of Kramer's suckers got tired of havin' Kramer on his back. He got himself a car and a gun, and he went on a shooting party. Good-by, Sy, say hello to the man with the horns and the pitchfork."

"Whoever did the shooting was pretty good, Danny. Only one shot was fired, and it took away half of Kramer's face. That doesn't sound like an amateur."

"There's lotsa amateurs who can shoot good," Danny said. "It don't mean a damn thing. Somebody wanted him dead pretty bad, Steve. And from what I can pick up, it ain't the gangs. Half the racket boys never even hearda Kramer. If you're workin' what he was workin', you do it alone. It's common arithmetic. If you work it with a part-ner, you have to split everything but the prison sentence."

"You've got no idea who he was milking?" Carella asked.

"If I knew, I'd have tried to get in on it myself," Danny said, smiling. "I'll try to find out. But the secret of extortion is just that: the secret. If too many people know about it, it ain't a secret any more. And if it ain't a secret, why should anybody pay off to protect it? I'll listen around, I'll go on the earie. But this is a tough thing to find out."

"What do you know about a man named Mario Torr?"

"Torr, Torr," Danny said. "Torr. It don't ring a bell."

"He took a fall for extortion in 1952," Carella said. "Got one-to-two on the state, paroled in fifty-three. Had a pre-vious arrest for blackmail. He's allegedly honestly em-ployed now, but he's interested in Kramer's death, claims he was a good friend of Kramer's. Know him?"

"It still don't ring," Danny said. "Maybe he really did go straight, who knows? Listen, miracles *can* happen, you know."

"Not often enough," Carella said. "Have you seen any imported talent around?"

"You're thinking Kramer was important enough to hire an out-of-town gun? Steve, believe me, this is crazy reasoning."

"Okay, okay. But is there any imported stuff around?"

"A hood from Boston. They call him Newton, cause that's where he's from."

"A gun?"

"I think he cooled a few, but you can't prove it by me. He ain't here for that, though."

"Why's he here?"

"They're tryina set up something between here and Boston. This Newton is just a messenger boy, so the Bigs don't hafta be seen together. He ain't the guy who cooled Kramer."

"Where is this Newton?"

"He's shacked in a hotel on The Stem, downtown. The Hotel Rockland. His last name's Hall." Danny chuckled. "He sounds like a girls' finishing school, don't he? Newton Hall." Danny chuckled again.

"You don't think he's worth looking up?" Carella asked.

"A waste of time. Listen, do what you want to do. I don't run the squad. But you're wastin' time. Let me listen a little. I'll buzz you if I get anything."

"What do I owe you?" Carella asked, reaching into his pocket.

"Wait'll I give you something," Danny said.

He shook hands and left the precinct. Carella walked over to Hawes's desk.

"Get your hat, Cotton," he said. "There's a bum I want to pick up."

Cotton Hawes was a recent transfer to the 87th Squad.

He was six feet two inches tall, and he weighed one hundred and ninety pounds bone dry. He had blue eyes and a square jaw with a cleft chin. His hair was red except for a streak over his left temple, where he had once been knifed and where the hair had curiously grown in white after the wound had healed. His straight nose was clean and unbroken, and he had a good mouth with a wide lower lip.

He also had good ears. He had been with the 87th for a very short time, but he had learned during those weeks that Steve Carella was a good man to listen to. When Carella spoke, Hawes listened. He listened to him all the way down to the Hotel Rockland in the police sedan. He listened to Carella when he flashed his tin at the desk clerk and asked for the key to Hall's room. He stopped listening only when Carella stopped talking, and Carella stopped talking the moment they stepped out of the elevator into the fourth-floor corridor.

There was, perhaps, no need for extreme caution. Unless Hall had been in on the Kramer kill, in which case there *was* need for extreme caution. In any case, both detectives drew their service revolvers. When they reached the door to Hall's room, they flanked it, and Carella's arm was the only portion of his body that presented a target as—standing to one side of the door—he inserted the key and rapidly twisted it. He flung open the door.

Newton Hall was sitting in a chair by the window, reading. He looked up with mild surprise on his face, and then his eyes dropped to the guns both men were carrying, and fear darted into those eyes.

"Police," Carella said, and the fear vanished as suddenly as it had appeared.

"Jesus," Hall said, "you scared me for a minute. Come on in. Put away the hardware, will you? Sit down."

"Get up, Hall," Carella said.

Hall rose from the chair. Hawes quickly frisked him.

"He's clean, Steve."

Both men holstered their guns.

"You got identification, I suppose," Hall said.

Carella was reaching for his wallet when Hall put out his hand to stop him. "Never mind, never mind," he said. "I was just asking."

"When'd you get to town, Hall?" Carella asked.

"Monday night," Hall said.

"The twenty-fourth?"

"Yeah. Listen, did I do something?"

"You tell us."

"What is it you want to know?"

"Where were you Wednesday night?" Hawes asked.

"Wednesday night?" Hall asked. "Let me see. Oh yeah, I was with a broad."

"What was her name?"

"Carmela."

"Carmela what?"

"Carmela Fresco."

"Where'd you go?"

"We stayed right here."

"All night?"

"Yeah."

"From what time to what time?"

"From about nine o'clock until the next morning. She left after breakfast."

"What'd you do all that time?" Hawes asked.

Hall grinned. "What do you think we did?"

"I don't know. You tell us."

Hall was still grinning. "We played Parchesi," he said.

"Leave the room at all during that time?"

"Nope. Here all night. I like Parchesi."

"Do you know a man named Sy Kramer?" Carella asked.

"Oh," Hall said. "That. I mighta known."

"Did you know him?"

"No. Never met him. I read about the killing in the newspapers."

"But you'd never met him?"

"Nope."

"Ever hear of him before?"

"Nope."

"Why'd you come here from Boston?"

"A little rest. See some of the shows. You know. Like that."

"What shows have you seen so far?" Hawes asked.

"None," Hall admitted. "It's pretty rough to get tickets, you know? Except for the longhair stuff. Who wants to see the longhair stuff? I like musicals. Songs, girls, that's for me. Goodtime Charlie, that's me." He snapped his fingers. "I got a friend who gets ice, you know what that is?"

"What is it?" Hawes asked.

"Free tickets. Not really free. Well, like they're paid for at box-office prices, but he sells them back a little higher, you know what I mean? The difference between the box-office price and what he gets is called ice. So he gets ice. Only he can't fix me up yet. Tickets are hard to get nowadays."

"And that's why you're here, right? To see a few shows."

"Yeah, and to take a rest."

"But you haven't seen any shows yet?"

"No."

"Have you rested?"

"Well, you know. . . ."

"Good-time Charlie, that's you," Carella said.

"Sure. Good-time Charlie, that's me."

"Where do we get in touch with this Carmela Fresco?"

"Why drag her into this?" Hall said.

"Have you got a better alibi?"

"No, but . . . She's just a kid. I know her, and we . . ."

"How old?" Hawes snapped.

"Nothing like that," Hall said. "She ain't underage, don't worry about that. I wasn't born yesterday. But she's a kid. You go around asking questions, you'll scare the hell out of her. Also, you might ruin a good thing for me."

"That's too bad," Carella said.

"What makes you think I had anything to do with the Kramer kill, anyway?" Hall said.

"Do you know who did?"

"That's a stupid question."

"Why?"

"Let's assume I *did* know, okay? Let's assume I know who hired some guys to *kill* Kramer. To *kill* him, now. Not to scare him or warn him or anything like that. To kill him. Cool him. Put him away. So these guys mean business, right? These guys ain't playing around. So do you think I would open my mouth on these guys who mean business, these guys who ain't playing around, these guys who hired some other guys to *kill* a guy? To *kill* him! Oh, you got to be real foolish to open your mouth on these rough fellows, don't you?"

"Are there some rough fellows in this, Hall?"

"I'll tell you the truth, I don't know. That's the truth. I don't usually assist bul—detectives, but this time I think you're barkin' up the wrong tree. If this was a rackets thing, I woulda heard about it. And I didn't hear nothin'."

"There's another possibility, of course," Hawes said.

"Yeah, what's that?"

"*You* could have killed Kramer."

"The only thing I killed on Wednesday night was a girl named Carmela Fresco. I send that kid, believe me. I send her! When she leaves me, she's killed. Dead. Unconscious." Hall smiled. "I tell you the truth, she kills me, too. It's a good arrangement."

"Like Murder, Incorporated," Carella said.

"Something like that. A mutual stoning society, so to

speak. We stone each other. Oh Jesus, does that kid stone me!"

"How do we reach her, Hall?"

"She's in the book."

"What's the number?"

"I told you. She's in the book."

"We can't read," Hawes said.

"Aw, come on, don't let me be the bastard, huh?" Hall said. "This way you can tell her you got it from the book. You'll be tellin' the truth."

"We don't mind lying a little," Carella said. "What's her number? We'll say we got it from the book."

Hall shrugged. "Hunter 1-3800," he said. "I wish you'd leave her out of it."

"You're not out of it yourself yet," Hawes told him.

"Oh, brother, I'm clean," Hall said. "I wish I was always so clean as I am on this one. I'm so clean, I glisten. I shine. I gleam."

"We'll see about that," Hawes said.

They started for the door. At the door, Carella turned.

"Oh. One more thing, Sun God."

"Yeah?" Hall said.

"Don't go back to Boston before checking with us."

"I'll be around," Hall said tiredly. "I got a few shows to see. Music, girls, you know. Good-time Charlie, that's—"

The door slammed on his sentence.

Carmela Fresco was somewhat shy and hesitant at the beginning. She was a good girl, she insisted, who would certainly never spend the night in any man's hotel room. What kind of girl did they think she was, anyway? Did she look like that kind of girl? Had this man Newton—or whatever his name was—said that she was that kind of girl?

Carella and Hawes were very patient with her.

The girl repeated her story again and again. She had certainly not been with this Newton—or whatever his name was—on Wednesday night or any other night. Over and over again, Carella and Hawes had her repeat the story of how she'd gone to a church bingo with her mother that night.

And then, in the middle of a sentence, she hesitated and then shouted, "That son of a bitch! Does he think I'm a slut, telling everybody in the world I spent the goddamn night with him?"

And that was it.

The reputation of Carmela Fresco may have emerged in a somewhat blemished condition. But the alibi of Newton Hall was clean, and glistening, and shining, and gleaming.

Hawes called him and told him he was free to go back to Boston any damn time he wanted to—the sooner the better, in fact.

Chapter 3

On the night of June twenty-sixth, when Sy Kramer was murdered, a passer-by came upon the body lying on the pavement and immediately telephoned the police. The call was taken by a patrolman who sat at one of the two Headquarters switchboards with a pad of printed forms before him. He took down the information exactly as it was excitedly delivered to him:

CENTRAL COMPLAINT DESK REPORT

TIME	DATE	CITY SECTION	PRECINCT
11:05 P.M.	JUN 26 1957	Isola	87th

RECEIVED BY	SWITCHBOARD OFFICER
Hq. Command	Ptl. R. Davis

ADDRESS *Barker Ave. & South 3rd* FLOOR ____

NAME OF COMPLAINANT *Andrew Pierson*

CRIME REPORTED *Homicide (?)*

DETAILS *Complainant discovered man bleeding on sidewalk. Says man is dead.*

DISPATCHER No._____ TIME_____

C.R.D. 16
2000L-60486 (53) •••••••••• 112

He rolled the complaint form into its metal carrier and sent it by pneumatic tube into the radio room, where a dispatcher put his number into the appropriate space, consulted the huge precinct map on the wall behind him, and then dispatched a radio motor-patrol car to the scene of the crime.

He indicated the time of the dispatch on the form, and then added it to the pile of forms on one side of his desk. The patrolman who'd taken the call meanwhile informed the Detective Division of the 87th Precinct, and asked them to report back if it was truly a homicide so that he could then inform Homicide South.

The detectives who caught the squeal were Carella and Hawes, and so the case was officially theirs.

They were, of course, free to call upon other members of the Squad for assistance if they needed it, provided Detective Lieutenant Byrnes—who commanded the Squad—felt he could spare those men. And Homicide South would begin its own investigation while noisily advising the 87th that homicide was not a precinct squad's cup of tea. In truth, whether the two homicide squads (North and South) chose to admit it or not, they would have been completely swamped had they tried to handle the city's flood of homicide cases unaided. So whereas they bore the official titles and whereas they made a lot of noise about squad interference in murder cases, they tacitly agreed that the majority of homicide cases *could* be handled (and *were*, in fact, being handled) by the detective squads of the precincts in which the murders had taken place. The role of the two homicide squads, except in rare cases, was usually advisory, sometimes supervisory. Busily, noisily, they went about trying to convince themselves that they alone were qualified to handle homicide cases. Secretly, quietly, they realized they were like job foremen watching other men digging a trench, watching other men doing the actual labor.

The case, then, for all actual purposes, belonged to Carella and Hawes.

They had been out of the office when Mario Torr arrived with his theories about the shooting, and so Kling had naturally spoken to the man, later passing on the information to his colleagues. At bull sessions in the office, he would feel free to air any theories he had about the slaying, putting his two cents into the pot. The men of the 87th Squad worked well together. Each had his two cents' worth to deliver on any case being investigated—and it doesn't take long for two cents from each man to add up to a sound dollar.

On Saturday, June twenty-ninth, Cotton Hawes—one of the two detectives officially investigating the untimely demise of Sy Kramer—went to bed with the erstwhile mistress of Kramer, and made an amazing discovery about himself.

He discovered that he could fall in and out of love with consummate ease. He discovered this personality defect—or asset, as the case might be—with some trepidation, some amusement, and some speculation.

Kramer's ex-mistress, he supposed, was partly to blame. But Hawes had never been a man to hide behind a woman's skirts, and he would not do so now. When it was all over, he accepted his equal share of the blame—or the credit, as the case might be—and congratulated himself upon what he considered an honorable seduction. He had used his shield as neither a threat nor an inducement. Cotton Hawes the *man* had gone to bed with this woman, not Cotton Hawes the *cop*. He had, in fact, even waited until he was off-duty before consummating the distinct and definite animal awakening he had felt that afternoon while questioning her.

The girl's name was Nancy O'Hara.

Her hair was red, but none of her friends or relations called her Scarlett. Passing strangers, passing drunks, had been known to say to her, "O'Hara, huh? Now, could it be *Scarlett* O'Hara?" as if they had originated the wittiest remark of the century. Nancy usually answered such devastating wit with a slightly embarrassed smile and the quietly spoken answer, "No, I'm *John* O'Hara. The writer."

She was, in truth, neither Scarlett O'Hara nor John O'Hara.

She was Nancy O'Hara, and she had been the mistress of Sy Kramer.

Cotton Hawes had fallen in love with her the moment she opened the door of her Jefferson Avenue apartment, even though she was not dressed in a manner that was conducive to falling in love. She was, in fact, dressed like a slob.

She was wearing dungarees, the bottoms of which were wet to the knee. She wore a man's dress shirt, the tails hanging over the dungarees, the sleeves rolled to her elbows. She had bright-green eyes, and her full mouth was on the edge of panic, and she didn't at all look like an extortionist's mistress, whatever an extortionist's mistress looks like.

She opened the door, and immediately said, "Thank God you're here! It's this way. Come with me."

Hawes followed her through a luxurious living room, and then into an equally luxurious bedroom, and then through that into a bathroom that—at the moment—had all the charm of a small swimming pool.

"What took you so long?" Nancy said. "A person could drown by the time—"

"What's the trouble?" he asked.

"I told you on the phone. I can't turn off the shower. Something's struck. The whole damn apartment'll float away unless we turn it off."

Hawes took off his jacket. Nancy glanced at the shoulder holster and the sturdy butt of the .38 protruding from the leather.

"Do you always carry a gun?" she asked.

"Always," he said.

She nodded soberly. "I always suspected plumbing was a hazardous profession."

Hawes had already reached into the tub. Grasping the knobs on the fixtures, he said, "They're stuck."

"Yes, I know."

"Did you call a plumber?"

"If you're not the plumber," she said, "you entered this apartment under false pretenses."

Hawes tugged at the stubborn fixtures. "I never said I was a plumber. I'm getting wet."

"What are you?"

"A cop."

"You can get right out of bathroom," Nancy said.

"Shhh, it's beginning to turn, I think."

"You're supposed to have a warrant before—"

"There it goes," Hawes said. "Now all I've got to—OW!" He pulled his hand back and began shaking it.

"What's the matter?"

"I must have turned off the cold water. I burned myself."

Steam was beginning to pour into the small bathroom.

"Well, do something," Nancy said. "For God's sake, you've made it worse."

"If I can turn up that nozzle . . ." Hawes said, half to himself. He reached up and directed the spray of hot water toward the far tile wall. "There." And then he began struggling with the hot-water knob. "It's giving," he said. "How'd you manage to get them stuck?"

"I was going to take a shower."

"In your dungarees?"

"I put these on after I called the plumber."

"There it goes," Hawes said. He twisted the knob, and the water suddenly stopped. "Phew."

Nancy looked at him. "You're soaking wet," she said.

"Yes." Hawes grinned.

She studied him, and then reluctantly said, "Well, take off your shirt. You can't walk around all dripping like that. I'll get you something to wear."

"Thanks," Hawes said. Nancy left the bathroom. He unstrapped the holster and laid it across the top of the toilet tank. Then he pulled his shirt out of his trousers and unbuttoned it. He was pulling his tee shirt over his head when Nancy came back.

"Here," she said. "It'll probably be small for you." She handed him a pale-blue, long-sleeved sports shirt with the monogram *SK* over the left breast pocket.

"Mr. Kramer's?" Hawes asked, putting on the shirt.

"Yes." Nancy paused. "That's an expensive shirt, imported from Italy. But I don't think he'll mind your wearing it."

Hawes put on the shirt and rolled up the sleeves. The shirt was tight across his broad chest, skimpy where his shoulders threatened the luxurious cloth. He picked up his jacket, his wet clothes, and his shoulder rig.

"Give me the clothes," she said. "I have a dryer."

"Thanks."

"You can sit in the living room," she told him.

"Thanks."

"There's whisky in the cabinet."

"Thanks."

She went into a small alcove off the kitchen. Hawes went into the living room and sat. He could hear her starting the automatic dryer. She came into the room and stood looking at him.

"What's your name?"

"Detective Hawes."

"Have you got a warrant, Mr. Hawes?"

"I only want to ask some questions, Miss O'Hara. I don't need a warrant for that."

"Besides, you did fix my shower." She had a sudden idea. "I better phone the super and tell him to call off the plumber. Excuse me a minute." She stopped on the way out of the room. "I better change my pants, too. Don't you want a drink?"

"Not allowed," Hawes said.

"Oh, bull," she answered, and left.

Hawes walked around the room. A framed picture of Sy Kramer was on the grand piano. A humidor with six pipes in it rested on a table near one of the easy chairs. The room was a masculine room. He felt quite at home in it, and, curiously, he began to admire the late Sy Kramer's expensive good taste.

When Nancy returned, she had tucked the man's shirt into a pair of striped tapered slacks.

"Typical petty officialdom," she said.

"Huh?"

"The super. I told him not to bother sending the plumber. He said, 'What plumber?' I could be lying drowned for all he cares. I owe you my thanks."

"You're welcome."

"Won't you have a drink?"

"No, thanks, I'm really not supposed to."

"Nobody does what he's supposed to these days," Nancy said. "What do you drink?"

"Scotch," he said.

"Sy had good Scotch, I understand. I never drink Scotch, but I understand it's good." She poured a glass for him. "Anything in it?"

"Just some ice."

She dropped the cubes into the glass, and then poured herself some gin over one ice cube. "Am I rushing the season?" she asked.

"What?"

"Gin."

"I don't think so."

She brought him his drink. "Here's to the plumbers of America," she said.

"Cheers."

They drank.

"What questions did you want to ask, Mr. Hawes?"

"Just some routine stuff."

"About Sy?"

"Yes."

"How'd you get to me?"

"Were you and he supposed to be a secret?" Hawes asked.

"No," she said. "I expected the police. I just wondered . . ."

"We asked around."

"Well, what do you want to know?"

"How long had you been living together?"

"Since last September."

"What happens now?"

Nancy shrugged. "The rent's paid up for next month. After that, I move."

"Where to?"

"Someplace." She shrugged again. "I'm"—she paused— "a dancer. I'll get work. I'll begin making the rounds again."

"How'd you meet Kramer?"

"Along The Stem. I'd been making the rounds one morning, and I was pooped. I stopped for a cup of coffee at one of the drugstores, a hangout for the kids in the business. Sy started talking to me at the counter. We began dating." Again she shrugged. "Here I am."

"Um-huh."

"Don't look so puritanical," Nancy said.

"Was I?"

"Yes. I wasn't exactly a pure-white lily when I met Sy. I'm twenty-seven years old, Mr. Hawes. I was born and raised in this city. I'm not a farm girl who was lured here by the bright lights. Sy didn't comb the hayseed out of my hair."

"No?"

"No. I'm a pretty good dancer, but a person gets tired as hell making those rounds. Do you know how many dancers there are in this town?"

"How many?"

"Plenty. For every chorus line, there are probably five hundred girls who answer the casting call. I had an idea once."

"Yes."

"I thought I'd lay my way to the top."

"Did it work?"

"I'm still unemployed," Nancy said. "Sy's proposition sounded like a good one. Besides, he was a nice guy. I liked him. I wouldn't have lived with him if I didn't like him. I've lived with starving actors in the Quarter and didn't like them half as much."

"Did you know he had a criminal record?"

"Yes."

"Did you know he was an extortionist?"

"No. Was he?"

"Yes."

"He told me he'd been in jail once because he'd got into a fight over a girl in a bar."

"How did he explain his income to you?"

"He didn't. And I never asked."

"Did he keep regular working hours?"

"No."

"And you never suspected he might be involved in something illegal?"

"No. Well, to be truthful, yes, I did. But I never asked him about it."

"Why not?"

"A man's business is *his* business. I don't believe in prying."

"Um-huh," Hawes said.

"You don't believe me?"

"I believe you. I was hoping you'd be able to give us a lead onto his victim or victims." Hawes shrugged. "But if you don't know anything about—"

"I don't." Nancy was thoughtful for a moment. "Where'd you get the white streak?"

"Huh? Oh." Hawes touched his hair. "I got knifed once."

"It's attractive." She smiled. "The very latest thing, you know."

"I try to keep in tune with the new fashions," Hawes said, returning the smile. "Do you have any idea how much money Kramer was maki'

"No. A lot, I suppos   nis apartment isn't exactly a coldwater flat."

"Hardly," Hawes said. "Do you know what the rental runs?"

"I think it's three-fifty a month."

Hawes whistled.

"Who invents these stories about crime not paying?" Nancy said.

"Does it?" Hawes asked.

"Well, look at—"

"Kramer died in a gutter," Hawes said flatly.

"But he lived in a penthouse," Nancy answered.

"I'd rather live in Calm's Point and die in bed."

"Do many cops die in bed?"

"Most of them," Hawes said. "Did Kramer have an address book?"

"Yes. Shall I get it for you?"

"Later. Any bankbooks?" Hawes paused. "Checkbooks?"

"One of each," Nancy said.

"A safety deposit box?"

"I don't think so."

"You're pretty, Miss O'Hara," Hawes said.

"I know," she answered.

"I know you know. That doesn't make you any less pretty."

"Has the routine questioning stopped?" she asked. "Are we ready to do the sex bit?"

"I—"

"You were beginning to sound like most agents and producers in this town. I thought cops were above that sort of stuff. Except cops on the vice squad."

"I didn't think you'd mind being told you're pretty," Hawes said. "I'm sorry."

"You're pretty, too," Nancy answered. "The compliment has been returned, now let's drop the bit. Are there any more questions?"

"Did Kramer ever entertain here?"

"Sometimes."

"What kind of friends did he have?"

"All kinds."

"Criminals?"

"I wouldn't know a forger if he signed a check for me."

"You must have listened to conversations."

"I did. Crimes were never discussed. The people Sy entertained seemed like respectable citizens with wives and children."

"Thieves have wives and children, too," Hawes said.

"I don't think these people were thieves. One was an architect, I think. Another a lawyer."

"Did Kramer have any interests besides his—ah—work?" Hawes asked.

"Like what?"

"Hobbies? Organizations? You know."

"He liked to hunt. He went on hunting trips every now and then."

"Where?"

"The mountains."

"Take you with him?"

"No. I don't like to kill animals."

"Did you and Kramer get along, Miss O'Hara?"

"Very well. Why?"

"Do you personally know any criminals, Miss O'Hara?"

"You mean did I hire the person who shot Sy?"

"If you prefer."

"No. I did not hire him, and I do not know any criminals. I know only one person connected with crime, and he is beginning to bore me."

Hawes smiled. "I'm sorry," he said. "I have to ask questions. That's what I'm paid for."

"Shall I get that stuff for you?"

"Please. It might help us. Or don't you care whether or not we find his murderers?"

Nancy thought this over gravely. "Sy's dead," she said simply. "Our relationship was a temporary one. I liked him a lot, and I suppose I'd like to see justice triumph. I'll help you in any way possible. Will I weep bitterly? No, I will not. Will I think of Sy six months from now? Probably not. Do I sound hard and cynical?"

"Yes."

"Perhaps it's because I am hard and cynical."

The words came from Hawes's mouth before he knew he was about to speak them. "You look soft and sentimental," he said.

"Here comes the sex bit again," she answered.

"Yes, here comes the sex bit. Will you get me the bankbook, the checkbook, and the address book, please?"

"Sure," she said. She rose and started out of the room. At the door she turned and said, "Maybe I will weep bitterly. I liked Sy."

"Good."

"And I suppose men always make passes. I suppose it's the nature of the beast."

"I suppose so," Hawes said.

"I shouldn't have squelched you."

"Maybe I was out of line."

"Maybe you weren't."

She looked at Hawes steadily.

"Miss O'Hara," he said, "I've never dated a redhead."

"No?"

"No. I'm leaving the office at six thirty tonight. Do you think we might have dinner together?"

"To find out more about Sy and his bad associates?"

"No. To find out more about you."

"I have a very hearty appetite. I'm an expensive date."

Hawes grinned. "I received my graft rake-off today," he said.

"I believe you."

"Can you be out of those dungarees by seven thirty?"

"I can," she said. "It's a question of whether I will."

"Will you?"

"Yes." She paused. "Don't expect . . ."

"I'm not."

"Okay."

She left the room to get the items he wanted.

They had dinner in one of the city's better restaurants. Nancy O'Hara was very pleasant company, and Cotton Hawes fell hopelessly in love with her. He would fall hopefully out of love with her by the next day, but for now she was the only woman in the universe. And so they ate a nourishing meal. And so they talked and laughed and drank. And so they went to a late movie. And so they went back to Nancy's apartment for a nightcap.

And so to bed.

Chapter 4

The passbook for the savings account looked like this:

	DATE	WITHDRWL	DEPOSIT	INT	BALANCE
A	10/23		21,000.00		21,000.00
1	1/7		9,000.00		30,000.00
2	4/11		15,000.00		45,000.00
	APR 1957			187.50	45,187.50

In acct. with: _Seymour Kramer_

The account had been started in October with the sum of $21,000. In January there had been an additional deposit of $9,000, and in April a third deposit of $15,000. The interest, computed on April first and indicated in the passbook at the time the April eleventh deposit had been made, was $187.50. Kramer had not made a withdrawal since the account had been opened.

The checking account was a working account. There were regular deposits and withdrawals. The deposits were usually made around the first of each month, give or take a week. The deposits were made in three unvarying amounts: $500, $300, and $1,100. The withdrawals were made in varying amounts—to pay bills and for pocket money. The savings account, it seemed, had been Kramer's nest egg. The checking account was the one that had sustained him in his daily pursuit of happiness, to the tune of $1,900 a month.

The bank, on Monday morning, July first, had two checks that were waiting to be deposited in Kramer's checking account. The checks had apparently been mailed together with a deposit slip on the afternoon Kramer had been killed. They had not reached the bank until Friday morning, had not been got to that afternoon, and so were still waiting for deposit on Monday.

Both checks were made payable to cash.

One check was in the amount of $500.

The other was in the amount of $300.

One was signed by a woman named Lucy Mencken.

The other was signed by a man named Edward Schlesser.

Both checks had been endorsed for deposit by Sy Kramer.

Lucy Mencken tried hard not to appear voluptuous. It was impossible. She wore a man-tailored suit and low walking shoes, and her long brown hair was pulled into a bun at the nape of her neck, and she tried to give the impression of a sedate exurban matron, but it was impossible.

Steve Carella happened to be married to a voluptuous woman. He knew all about voluptuousness or voluptuity or whatever Webster called it; Carella had never taken the time to look it up. He knew that his wife, Teddy, was voluptuous, and using her as a measuring rod, he knew there wasn't a woman alive who could fool him into thinking she was *not* voluptuous simply by wearing a dowdy-looking suit and Army shoes. In the terraced back yard of the exurban estate, overlooking the swimming pool in the distance, Carella sat with Lucy Mencken and wondered why she wore Army shoes.

The trees rustled with a gentle breeze, cool for July. He could remember the summer before and the sweltering routine of working in an inferno with a cop hater loose. It would have been nice, last summer, to have had access to a pool the size of the one on the Mencken estate. He sat watching Lucy Mencken as she sipped her gin and tonic. She held the glass with complete familiarity, a woman at home with her surroundings, a woman at ease with luxury. The luxury made Carella somewhat uncomfortable. He felt like a man who'd come to give an estimate on how much it would cost to prune the trees near the gatehouse.

The fact that she was voluptuous disturbed him, too. She moved with complete ease within the rounded length of her body, but the clothing was a complete contradiction and it emphasized rather than denied the ripeness of her flesh. He wondered what a single man's reaction to Mrs. Mencken would be. He wondered, for example, how things would have worked out if *he'd* gone to see Edward Schlesser and sent Cotton Hawes to meet Mrs. Mencken. From what Hawes had told him, Nancy O'Hara had turned out to be a beautiful girl. And now there was Lucy Mencken. Sometimes it went like that, he supposed. A case bursting with beauty. Idly he wondered what it was like to be single. Happily he thanked God he was married.

"What was your relationship with a man named Sy Kramer, Mrs. Mencken?" he asked.

Lucy Mencken sipped at her drink. "I don't know anyone named Sy Kramer," she said. In the distance Carella could hear shouting and laughter from the pool.

"Seymour Kramer, then," he said.

"I don't know any Seymour Kramer, either."

"I see," Carella said. "Did you know that Mr. Kramer is dead?"

"How would I know that?"

"It was in the newspapers."

"I rarely read the newspapers. Except where it concerns my family."

"Does your family often make headlines?" Carella asked.

"My husband is in politics," Mrs. Mencken said. "He will be running for the state senate this fall. His name often appears in the newspapers, yes."

"How long have you been married, Mrs. Mencken?"

"Twelve years," she answered.

"And how old are your children?"

"Davey is ten, and Greta is eight."

"What did you do before you were married?"

"I modeled," she said.

"Fashion?"

"Yes," she answered.

"Vogue, Harper's Bazaar? Like that?"

"Yes."

"Do you do any modeling now, Mrs. Mencken?"

"No. I stopped modeling when I got married. Being a wife and a mother is enough of a career."

"What was your maiden name?"

"Lucy Mitchell."

"Is that the name under which you modeled?"

"I modeled under the name of Lucy Starr Mitchell."

"About twelve years ago, is that right?"

"Twelve, thirteen years ago, yes."

"Is that when you met Sy Kramer?" Carella asked.

Mrs. Mencken did not bat an eyelid. "I don't know anyone named Sy Kramer," she said.

"Mrs. Mencken," Carella said gently, "you sent him a check, dated June twenty-fourth, for five hundred dollars."

"You must be mistaken."

"Your signature is on that check."

"There are other Lucy Menckens in the world, I'm sure," she said.

"You *do* have a checking account with the Federal Savings and Loan of Peabody, do you not?"

"Yes."

"There is only one Lucy Mencken who has an account with that bank, Mrs. Mencken."

"If that's the case, the check was forged. I'll have it stopped at once."

"The bank has verified your signature, Mrs. Mencken."

"It still could have been forged. That's the only explanation I have for it. I don't know anybody named Sy Kramer or Seymour Kramer or *any* Kramer at all. The check was obviously forged. I'll call the bank and have it stopped."

"Mrs. Mencken . . ."

"In fact, I'm grateful to you for calling it to my attention."

"Mrs. Mencken, Sy Kramer is dead. You no longer have anything to fear."

"Why should I have anything to fear? My husband is a very powerful man."

"I don't know what you had to fear, Mrs. Mencken, but Kramer is dead. You can tell me. . . ."

"Then he won't miss the check if I put a stop-payment on it."

"Why was he blackmailing you, Mrs. Mencken?"

"Who?"

"Sy Kramer. Blackmail or extortion. Why?"

"I don't know what you're talking about."

"His checking account shows a monthly deposit of five hundred dollars, along with other deposits, of course. Your check was made out for five hundred dollars. Why did you send Sy Kramer a check for five hundred dollars each month?"

"I don't know what you're talking about."

"May I see your checkbook stubs, Mrs. Mencken?"

"Certainly not."

"May I see your canceled checks?"

"No."

"I can get a search warrant."

"That's just what you'll have to do, then, Mr. Carella. My checkbook and my canceled checks are private. Not even my husband questions me on what I spend or how I spend it."

"I'll come back with a warrant," Carella said, rising.

"Do you really expect to find anything when you return, Mr. Carella?" she asked.

"I suppose not," he said wearily. He looked at her searchingly. "You don't dress like an ex-fashion model, Mrs. Mencken."

"Don't I?"

"No."

"This suit cost three hundred and fifty dollars, Mr. Carella."

"That's a lot of money to hide behind."

"Hide?"

"Mrs. Mencken, a man was murdered. He was not what you might consider an ideal citizen, but he was nonetheless murdered. We are trying to find his murderer. I wish you had helped me. We'll find out what we want to know, anyway. You can hide your checks and your stubs, and you can hide yourself behind that expensive suit, but we'll find out."

"Mr. Carella, you are being impertinent."

"Forgive me."

Lucy Mencken rose, moving with easy grace within the shapeless suit.

"The children are in the pool alone," she said. "Were you leaving, Detective Carella?"

"I was leaving," Carella said tiredly, "but I'll be back."

The check lay on the desk between them.
The legend on the frosted-glass door read, SCHLESSER'S

SOFT DRINKS. The man behind the desk was Edward Schlesser, a balding man in his early fifties. He wore a dark-blue suit and a yellow weskit. He wore black-rimmed bop glasses. The glasses covered blue eyes, and the eyes studied the check on the desk.

FAIRFAX, CONN._____ June 23 _____ 19 57 No. 833_____

THE FIRST NATIONAL BANK & TRUST CO. $\frac{51-106}{211}$

PAY TO THE ORDER OF____ CASH _____ $ 300.00

Three hundred and no/100------------------------DOLLARS

Edward Schlesser

Insured against fraudulent alteration

"Is that your check, Mr. Schlesser?" Cotton Hawes asked.

Schlesser sighed. "Yes," he said.

"Did you send it to a man named Seymour Kramer?"

"Yes."

"Why?"

"What difference does it make? He's dead."

"That's why I'm here," Hawes said.

"It's over now," Schlesser said. "Are you like a priest? Or a doctor? Does what I tell you remain confidential?"

"Certainly. In any case, it won't get outside the department."

"How do I know I can trust you?"

"You don't. Did you trust Sy Kramer?"

"No," Schlesser said. "If I'd trusted him, I wouldn't have been sending him checks."

"This wasn't the first check?"

"No, I—" Schlesser stopped. "Who will you tell this to?"

"Two people. My partner on the case, and my immediate superior."

Schlesser sighed again. "I'll tell you," he said.

"I'm listening, sir."

"I run this business," Schlesser said. "It's not a big one, but it's growing. There's competition, you know. It's hard to buck the big companies. But my business is growing, all the time. I've got money in the bank, and I've got a nice house in Connecticut. My business is here, but I live in Connecticut. I make good soft drinks. Our orange is particularly good. Do you like orange?"

"Yes."

"I'll give you a case when you leave. If you like it, tell your friends."

"Thank you," Hawes said. "What about Kramer?"

"We had an accident a little while ago. In the bottling plant. Not too serious, but a thing like that, if it gets around. . . . This is a small business. We're just beginning to make a mark, people are just beginning to recognize our bottle and the name Schlesser. A thing like this. . ."

"What happened?"

"Somehow, don't ask me how, a freak accident—a mouse got bottled into one of the drinks."

"A mouse?" Hawes asked incredulously.

"A tiny little thing," Schlesser said, nodding. "A field mouse. The bottling plant is in a field, naturally. Somehow the mouse got in, and somehow he got into one of the bottles, and somehow it went through the plant and was shipped to our distributors. A bottle of sarsaparilla as I recall."

Hawes wanted to smile, but apparently this was a matter of extreme seriousness to Schlesser.

"Somebody bought the bottle of soda. It was the large family size, the economy size. This person claimed he drank some of the soda and got very sick. He threatened to sue the company."

"For how much?"

"A hundred and twenty-five thousand dollars."

Hawes whistled. "Did he win the case?"

"It never got to court. The last thing we wanted was a trial. We settled for twenty-five thousand dollars out of court. I was glad to have it over with. There wasn't a peep in the papers about it. It could have ruined me. People remember things like that. A mouse in a bottle of soda? Jesus, you can be ruined!"

"Go on," Hawes said.

"About a month after we'd settled, I got a telephone call from a man who said he knew all about it."

"Kramer?"

"Yes. He threatened to turn a certain document over to the newspapers unless I paid him money to withhold it."

"Which document?"

"The original letter that had come from the claimant's attorney, the letter telling all about the mouse."

"How'd he get it?"

"I don't know. I checked the files, and sure enough it was gone. He wanted three thousand dollars for the letter."

"Did you pay him?"

"I had to. I'd already paid twenty-five thousand dollars to keep it quiet. Another three wouldn't hurt me. I thought it would be the end of it, but it wasn't. He'd had photostated copies of the letter made. He asked for an additional three hundred dollars a month. Each time I sent him my check, he'd send back another photostated copy. I figured he'd run out sooner or later. It doesn't matter now, anyway. He's dead."

"He may have friends," Hawes said.

"What do you mean?"

"A partner, a cohort, someone who'll pick up right where he left off."

"In that case, I'll keep paying the three hundred dollars a month. It comes to thirty-six hundred dollars a year. That's not so much. I spend sixty thousand dollars a year advertising my soft drinks. All that would go down the drain if that letter got to the newspapers. So another thirty-six hundred a year isn't going to kill me. If Kramer has a partner, I'll keep paying."

"Where were you on the night of June twenty-sixth, Mr. Schlesser?" Hawes asked.

"What do you mean? You mean the night Kramer was killed?"

"Yes."

Schlesser began laughing. "That's ridiculous. Do you think I'd kill a man for three hundred dollars a month? A lousy three hundred dollars a month?"

"Suppose, Mr. Schlesser," Hawes said, "that Kramer had decided to release that letter to the newspapers no matter *how* much you paid him? Suppose he just decided to be a mean son of a bitch?"

Schlesser did not answer.

"Now, Mr. Schlesser. Where were you on the night of June twenty-sixth?"

Chapter 5

The photographer's name was Ted Boone.

His office was on swank Hall avenue, and he knew the men of the 87th because a month ago they had investigated the murder of his ex-wife. The call to Boone was made by Bert Kling, who knew him best. And Kling was asking for a favor.

"I hate to bother you," he said, "because I know how busy you are."

"Has this got something to do with the case?" Boone asked.

"No, no," Kling said, "that's closed—until the trial, at any rate."

"When will that be?"

"I think it's set for August."

"Will I be called?"

"I don't know, Mr. Boone. That's up to the district attorney." He paused, remembering Boone's young daughter. "How's Monica?"

"She's fine, thanks. She'll be coming to live with me this month."

"Give her my love, will you?"

"I'll certainly do that, Mr. Kling."

There was a long pause.

"The reason I'm calling . . ." Kling said.

"Yes?"

"We're working on something now, and I thought you might be able to help. You do a lot of fashion photography, don't you?"

"Yes."

"Did you ever use a model named Lucy Starr Mitchell?"

"Lucy Starr Mitchell." Boone thought for a moment. "No, I don't think so. Do you know which agency she's with?"

"No."

"Is she hot now?"

"What do you mean?"

"Well, models have their ups and downs. They're hot for a while, and then they cool off. Their faces get too well known. People begin to say, 'Oh, there's that exquisite redhead!' instead of 'Oh, there's an exquisite dress.' Do you understand me? The model begins selling herself instead of the product."

"I see."

"But the name doesn't register with me. If she were active now, I'd recognize it. I use most of the topflight girls."

"I think she was modeling about twelve or thirteen years ago," Kling said.

"Oh. Then I wouldn't know her. I haven't been in the business that long."

"How would I find out about her, Mr. Boone?"

"You can call the registries. They've got back records. They can pinpoint her in a minute. Meanwhile, if you like, I'll ask around. I have friends who've been at this much longer than I. If they used her, they'll probably remember."

"I'd appreciate that."

"What was the number there again?"

"Frederick 7-8024."

"Okay, I'll check into it."

"Thank you, Mr. Boone."

"Not at all," he said, and he hung up.

The telephone would occupy Bert Kling for the rest of the afternoon. He would learn nothing from it. Or at any rate, he would learn a negative something.

He would learn that none of the model registries had ever carried a girl named Lucy Starr Mitchell.

Meyer Meyer did not mind being a tail, especially when the tail was tacked to the behind of Lucy Mencken. Lucy Mencken had a very nice behind.

On July second, Meyer was parked up the street from the Mencken house in a plain pale-blue sedan. At 8:05 A.M., a man answering the description of Charles Mencken left the house. At 9:37, Lucy Mencken went to the garage, backed out a red MG, and headed for the town of Peabody. Meyer followed her.

Lucy Mencken went to the hairdresser, and Meyer waited outside.

Lucy Mencken went to the post office, and Meyer waited outside.

Lucy Mencken had lunch at a quaint exurban teashop, and Meyer waited outside.

She went into a dress shop at 1:04.

By 2:15, Meyer began to suspect the awful truth. He got out of the sedan, walked into the shop, and then through it to the other side. As he'd suspected, there was another doorway at the far end of the shop. Lucy Mencken, by accident or design, had shaken her tail. Meyer drove back to the Mencken house. He could see the garage at the far end of the curving driveway. The red MG was not in it. Sighing heavily, he sat back to await her return.

She did not check in until 6:15.

Meyer went to dinner and then phoned Lieutenant Byrnes. Shamefacedly, he admitted that an exurban housewife had shaken him for five hours and eleven minutes.

The lieutenant listened patiently. Then he said, "Stick with it. She's probably home for the night. In any case, Willis'll be out to relieve you soon. What do you suppose she did during those five hours?"

"She could have done anything," Meyer said.

"Don't take it so big," Byrnes said. "Peabody hasn't reported any homicides yet."

Meyer grinned. "I'll be expecting Willis."

"He'll be there," Byrnes said, and he hung up.

Meyer went back to his vigil in the sedan. At 9:30 P.M., Willis relieved him. Meyer went home to bed. His wife, Sarah, wanted to know why he looked so down in the mouth.

"I'm a failure," Meyer said. "Thirty-seven years old and a failure."

"Go to sleep," Sarah said. Meyer rolled over. He did not once suspect that he himself had been tailed that afternoon, or that he'd led his follower directly to the home of Lucy Mencken.

It was Wednesday morning, July third.

A week had gone by since Sy Kramer had been shot from an automobile. The police had not learned very much during that week. They now knew where the monthly $500 and $300 deposits had originated. There was also a monthly $1,100 deposit in Kramer's working account, but they had not yet learned from whom that had come—and possibly they would never learn.

Nor did they know where the huge sums deposited in the other account had come from.

A check of Kramer's living habits had disclosed to the police that his taste was expensive, indeed. His suits were all hand-tailored, as were those of his shirts that had not been imported. His apartment had been furnished by a high-priced decorator. His whisky was the best money could buy. He owned two automobiles, a Cadillac convertible and a heavy-duty station wagon. The acquisitions were all apparently new ones, and this presented a puzzling aspect to the case.

The monthly deposits in Kramer's working account totaled $1,900. The withdrawals kept steady pace with the deposits. Kramer liked to live big, and he had been spending close to $500 a week. But the sum of $45,187.50 in the other account had not been touched. How, then, had he managed to buy the two automobiles, to pay for the furniture and the decorator, to afford the closetful of suits and coats?

How do you buy things without money?

You don't.

The Cadillac agency from which Kramer had purchased the automobile reported that it had been purchased during the latter part of the preceding September, and that Kramer had paid for it in cold, hard cash. The Buick station wagon had been purchased on the same day from an agency across the street in Isola's Automobile Row. Again, the purchase had been made in cash.

Kramer had rented his apartment in September. He had paid for the furniture and the decorator in cash. The total bill had come to $23,800. His suits had been ordered in September, delivered in October. They had cost him $2,000 —and he had paid for them with green United States currency.

Kramer, in short, had barefootedly run through $36,000 in cash in less than a month—and had managed to acquire a lovely mistress named Nancy O'Hara during that same wild spending spree. And then, on October twenty-third, he had deposited the staggering amount of $21,000 in his bank account!

From where had that original $36,000 come?

And from where had the subsequent deposits of $21,000 in October, $9,000 in January, and $15,000 in April come?

And had that $15,000 deposit been intended as the last

one? Or had more payments been scheduled to come? *Who* had been making the payments? Who had already paid a total of $81,000, and had this person been let off the hook only because Kramer was now dead?

And had not the extortion of $81,000 been sufficient reason for murder?

The body of Sy Kramer lying in the morgue seemed to indicate that it had indeed been reason enough.

The grand and glorious Fourth came in with a bang.

Some of the bulls of the 87th had the holiday off; the rest had to work. There was plenty to keep them occupied. In cooperation with the uniformed cops of the precinct, they tried to keep the day a safe and sane one. It was not.

Despite the city's law against fireworks, the importers had been busy, and everyone from six to sixty stood ready and anxious to apply a match to a fuse and then to stand back with his fingers in his ears. A kid on South Thirtieth lost an eye when another kid hurled a cherry bomb at his face. On Culver Avenue, two boys were shooting skyrockets from the roof. One fell over the edge and died the instant he hit the pavement.

It was not a very hot Fourth—there had been hotter Fourths—but it was a very noisy one. The noise was an excellent cover for those citizens who wanted to fire revolvers. You couldn't tell an exploding firecracker from an exploding .32 without a program, and nobody was selling programs that day. The police were busy chasing kids with fireworks, and turning off fire hydrants, and trying to stop burglaries that were being committed under cover of all the confusion and all the noise. The police were busy watching sailors who came uptown for a piece of exotica and very often went back downtown with a piece of their skulls missing. The police were busy watching the teen-age kids, who, now that school was over, now that time lay heavily on their hands, now that the asphalt streets and the concrete towers cradled them with boredom, now that there was nothing to do and plenty of time to do it in, were anxious for excitement, anxious for kicks, anxious for a little clean-living adolescent sport. They roamed the streets, and they roamed Grover Park, spoiling for action, and so the cops were kept busy.

Everyone was celebrating but the cops.

The cops were cursing because they had to work on a goddamn holiday.

Each of them wished he'd become a fireman.

At the firehouse in the 87th Precinct territory, the gongs were ringing and the men were sliding down poles and grabbing for helmets, because there'd be more damn fires today than on any other day of the year.

And each of the firemen wished he'd become a cop.

Chapter 6

Hal Willis was a detective 3rd/grade.

He earned $5,230 a year.

He earned this whether he was being shot at by a thief, or whether he was typing up a report in triplicate back at the squad. He earned it even when he was tailing a woman who tried to hide the swell of her curves by wearing potato-sack suits. The potato-sack suits, he supposed, made it interesting—like watching a stripper who never took off her clothes.

I am getting sick, he thought. There *are* no strippers who never take off their clothes.

In any case, and in any sense of the word, he did not mind the tail on Lucy Mencken. It had been agreeable work thus far, and he could not imagine how this charming housewife with a peekaboo body could possibly have shaken Meyer. Meyer is getting old, he thought. We'll have to put him out to pasture. We'll have to make him a stud bull. He will become the sire of a proud line of law-enforcement officers. They will erect a statue to him in Grover Park. The chiseled lettering at the base of the statue will read, MEYER MEYER, SIRE.

Sick, Willis thought. Sick, for sure.

He was a small man, Willis, barely clearing the five-foot-eight minimum-height requirement for policemen. Among the other detectives of the squad, he looked like a midget. But his deceptive height and his deceptively small bone structure did not fool any of the bulls who worked with him. There were not many men on the squad who wanted to fool with Willis. He was, you see, expert in the ways of judo. Hal Willis could, if you will allow your imagination to soar for a moment, seize the trunk of a charging elephant and—within a matter of seconds—cause that beast to sail through the air and land on his back with possible injury to his spinal column. Such was the might and the power of Hal Willis. Along more prosaic lines, and during the mundane pursuit of his chosen profession, Willis had disarmed thieves, dislocated bones, dispensed severe punishment, dispelled foolish notions about small men, disturbed virile giants who suddenly found themselves flat on their asses, dismayed crooks who did not realize bones could break so easily, and discovered that judo—good, clean fun that it was—could also become a way of life.

Weight and balance, that was the secret. Fulcrum and lever. Wait for your opportunity, seize it, and you had the world on its back.

Lucy Mencken was not, at the moment, on her back—although the thought, in all honesty, had often crossed Willis' mind since he'd begun tailing her. He had been warned by Carella, and later by Meyer, that Mrs. Mencken bore all the characteristics of a camouflaged munitions dump. Both Carella and Meyer were respectable married men who rarely, if ever, thought lewd, lascivious, or obscene thoughts. If they had seen fit to warn Willis about the necessity for keeping his mind on his work, then Mrs. Mencken was indeed highly explosive.

He had, at first, been disappointed. The woman who emerged from the house in Peabody looked more like a dowdy librarian than a bawdy libertine. It was after he'd been tailing her for a while that he began to appreciate the warnings of his colleagues. It was the most annoying damned thing, not that it wasn't also pleasant. The woman wore a suit that had surely been manufactured by Omar the tent maker. And yet, beneath that suit, there was the suggestion of vibrant flesh. The suggestion became more than that when the material tightened over her thigh as she stepped from her automobile, or molded the persistent flesh when she stooped to pick up her dropped purse. Lucy Mencken, no matter how she dressed, was voluptuous. And Willis did not at all mind tailing her, except that it was difficult to concentrate.

The tail, that morning of July fifth, led him directly to the Peabody railroad station. Willis had not anticipated this. He hastily parked the police sedan alongside the red MG and followed Lucy into the waiting room. He hoped to get to the ticket window in time to overhear her destination, but she was just turning away from the counter as he entered the waiting room. He didn't know whether she'd be heading north or south. South led to the city. North led to the next state and then beyond and beyond and beyond.

For all he knew, Lucy Mencken could be heading for Canada, or the North Pole, where she planned to sell bootleg whiskey to the Eskimos. Willis shrugged and went to the magazine stand, where he bought a copy of *Manhunt*. Under guise of reading the magazine, he watched Lucy Mencken.

He was amazed by the number of men she fooled. Surely it did not take a detective to know what the baggy linen suit concealed. Surely John Doe could look at her face and detect sensuality despite the severe hairdo and the absence of makeup. And yet, hardly a man in the waiting room turned for a second look at her. Even when she sat and crossed her legs—and there was, for a moment, the flash of thigh, the exalted glimpse of well-turned knee and calf, before her hand lowered the skirt like a linen curtain—none of the men in the waiting room seemed to care very much. Willis shook his head sadly. We are raising a generation of unobservant, impotent robots, he thought. Thank God for Meyer Meyer, Sire.

He could hear a train in the distance. Lucy Mencken looked at her watch, and then rose from the bench. Willis followed her onto the platform. She was, then, taking the southbound train. The last stop would be the city. Was that her destination, or would she get off at one of the stations along the line?

The train roared into the station, hissing steam, sounding its horn. A rush of air caught at Lucy's skirt. She backed away slightly, holding the skirt about her legs in a completely feminine gesture. She boarded the train and went directly to a smoking car. Willis followed her, and sat across the aisle and several seats behind her. When the conductor came around, he bought a round-trip ticket to the city. Then he sat back and read his detective magazine, glancing up every now and then to make sure Lucy had not moved.

She did not move until the train reached the city. Then she rose and disembarked.

This is great, Willis thought. We send a tail out to Peabody, and she leads the tail back to the city. Women, women.

He did not enjoy being back in the city. The city was a hell of a lot hotter than the exurbs had been. He cursed his bad luck, and stuck with Lucy Mencken. She caught a cab just outside the station. Willis got into the cab behind hers. He flashed his shield and told the cabbie not to lose her.

The cabbie did not. Lucy Mencken's cab cut through the crosstown traffic heading toward the River Harb. It pulled up in front of an office building on Independence Avenue in midtown Isola. Willis paid his hackie and went into the building after her. He had to run across the lobby in order to get into the same elevator with her.

She wore no perfume. He was standing close enough to her to detect that. He was standing close enough to see that her eyes were a clear blue flecked with tiny chips of white. He was standing close enough to see that her nose was spattered with freckles, and he suddenly wondered if she had originally been a farm girl.

"Eight," the elevator operator said.

Lucy stepped forward. Willis stepped forward with her. The doors slid open. Lucy stepped into the corridor. Willis waited until she was out of the car, and then followed. He made a great show of studying the numbers on each door he approached, as if he were looking for a specific office. Lucy walked directly to the end of the hall, opened a frosted-glass door, and entered. Willis waited a decent interval, and then went to the end of the hall. The lettering on the door said:

806

PATRICK BLIER

Photographers' Representative

Willis moved away from the door. He walked back to the elevator banks, and then flipped open his pocket pad and jotted down the number and name that had been on the door. He rang for the elevator and went down to the lobby. He checked the building to make sure there was only one entrance, and then went to the phone booths from which he could watch the elevators. Rapidly he dialed Frederick 7-8024.

"Eighty-seventh Precinct, Sergeant Murchison," the voice answered.

"Dave, this is Willis. Is Hawes upstairs?"

"Hold on a second, Hal. I'll check."

Willis waited.

"Eighty-seventh Squad, Detective Hawes," Hawes said.

"Cotton, this is Hal."

"Hi. How's the tail?"

"Fine. You should see it."

"Pretty?"

"A diamond, once you chip away the coal."

"Where are you?"

"In the city."

"Where's she?"

"1612 Independence Avenue. That's below the Square, midtown. She's in Room 806 with a quote photographers' representative unquote named Patrick Blier. Shall I hit him or maintain the tail?"

"Stay with her, Hal. Buzz me when she leaves, and I'll go down to see him."

"I'll leave the message with the desk," Willis said. "I won't have time to exchange cordialities or I'll lose her. She travels like a bunny."

"Okay. I'll ask Dave to let me know as soon as he gets your call. Stay with her, Hal."

"I'd love to," Willis said.

"You horny bastard."

"Horny? I'm red-blooded."

"I'm tired-blooded," Hawes said. "I'll be waiting for your call."

Patrick Blier, Photographers' Representative, was a bald man with a hooked nose. The first impression he gave was of a giant bald eagle. He sat behind his desk in a cubbyhole office the walls of which were covered with photographs of girls in various stages of dress and undress. A metal plaque on his desk announced the fact that he was *Mr.* P. Blier, in case anyone should accidentally think he was Miss or Mrs. P. Blier. To further eliminate doubt, Patrick Blier wore a transparent sports shirt, short-sleeved, and his chest was matted with thick black hair. His arms curled with the same black hair. A lesser man might have cracked under the pressure of all that hair everywhere but on the head. Patrick Blier didn't seem to care. He was bald, so he was bald. So what?

"So what do *you* want?" he asked Hawes when he stepped into the office.

"Didn't your receptionist tell you?"

"She said a detective was here. You a city cop or a private eye?"

"City."

"I get a lot of private eyes. They want my clients to take pictures for divorce cases. I explain to them that I ain't in the habit of breaking down bedroom doors. Private eyes are disgusting. Ain't nothing sacred? What do you want?"

"Some answers.'

"You got the questions?"

"Loads of them."

"Speak. I'm busy. I got requests up to here. I'm gonna have to get a bigger office, so help me God. Phones ringing all day long. Editors coming up day and night. Models pestering me. Jesus, what a rat race. What do you want? Speak. I'm busy."

"Why was Lucy Mencken here?"

"Who the hell is Lucy Mencken?"

"She was here a little while ago."

"You're nuts. Lucy Men—you mean Mitchell? You mean Lucy Mitchell? Is that who you mean?"

"Yes."

"So where the hell did you get this Mencken from? Say what you mean, will you? I'm busy."

"Why was she here?"

"Why, what'd she do?"

"Nothing."

"Then why should I tell you?"

"Why not?"

"First tell me what she done."

"Blier, I don't have to bargain with you. I asked a question. I'll ask it one more time. Why was she here, and what did she want?"

Blier studied Hawes for a long moment.

"You think you scare me?" he said at last.

"Yes," Hawes answered.

"You're right, you know that? You scare the hell out of me. Where the hell did you get that white hair? You look like the wrath of God, I swear to God. Jesus, I'd hate to meet you in a dark alley. Boy!"

"Why was she here?"

"She wanted some pictures."

"What kind of pictures?"

"Cheesecake."

"What was she going to do with them?"

"Paste them in her scrapbook, I guess. How the hell do I know? Do I care what a dame does with her own pictures? What do I care?"

"These were pictures of *her?*"

"Sure. Who'd you think? Marilyn Monroe, maybe?"

"What kind of pictures?"

"I told you. Cheesecake."

"Nude?"

"Some were nude. The rest were almost nude."

"How nude is *almost* nude?"

"Pretty nude. As nude as you can get without getting nude. As a matter of fact, nuder than if she was entirely nude, if you know what I mean."

"Who took these pictures?"

"One of my clients."

"Why?"

"To try to sell, what do you think? I sell to all the men's magazines. I handle other stuff, too, not only cheesecake. I don't want you to get the idea I only handle cheesecake. I do photographic essays. That is, I handle them. My clients shoot the actual stories."

"Which client took these pictures of Lucy Mitchell?"

"A guy named Jason Poole. He's a good man. Top-notch. Even these pictures were good, and he took them a long time ago."

"How long ago?"

"Ten, twelve years ago."

"Which?"

"How do I know? Who remembers that far back? She walked into the office today, I thought I was seeing a ghost."

"I'm not sure I'm following you, Blier. Suppose we start from the beginning."

"Oh my God, I'm busy. How can I go way back to the beginning?"

"By going there," Hawes said. "I'm busy, too, Blier. I'm busy investigating a homicide."

"That's murder?"

"That's murder."

"She done it?"

"Start from the beginning, Blier."

"The beginning was about ten, twelve years ago. Maybe longer. Let me think a minute." He thought a moment. "The war was just over. When was that?"

"1945."

"Yeah. No, wait a minute, the war wasn't over yet. The first war, the one with the bastard. *That* was over."

"You mean Hitler?"

"Who else? That one was over. We still had to clean up

the Pacific. Anyway, it was around then—1944, 1945.
Around then. I was sitting in the office alone. I didn't even
have a receptionist at the time. Just me. I had an office, I
wanted to change my mind I had to go outside to do it.
That's how big it was." Blier laughed at his own devastating
humor. "I was eating a sandwich. Pastrami on rye, from
Cohen's. Delicious pastrami. In walks this doll. An absolute
doll. A doll you could die with. With this doll, you could
put me on a desert island for the rest of my natural life
without food and water, so help me. Just her alone, and I'm
a happy man. That's the kind of a doll she was."

"Lucy Mitchell?" Hawes asked.

"Who else? With straw sticking out of her ears. Straight
from the farm, and milk-fed. Oh mister please, I get weak.
These big blue eyes, and this body, this body sings, it plays
sonatas, it's an orchestra with strings, Jesus I get weak. She
wants to model. She says she wants to model. I say did you
ever model? She says no she never modeled but she wants
her picture in magazines. I visualize a fortune in pinups. I
can see this doll decorating barracks from here to Tokyo.
I can even see her decorating *Japanese* barracks! Her I
wouldn't even deny the enemy, the bastards. But her
I wouldn't deny them. I send her up to see Jason Poole. He
takes a string of pictures. He can't stop the shutter from
clicking. Click, click, he shoots away all night long."

"Go on," Hawes said.

"He gets these marvelous pictures of this marvelous doll
with this body that makes concrete limp. I can visualize a
fortune. So what happens?"

"What happens?" Hawes asked.

"Next week I'm out of business. Some snotty underage
dame sues me for selling cheesecake for which she gave me
permission to sell. How was I supposed to know she's underage? I've got these lovely pictures of Lucy Mitchell, but
I ain't got no office any more because this other snotty
dame sued me out of existence."

"What happened to the pictures?"

"I don't know. Things got shuffled around. When I
opened the new office, the pictures were gone. I never seen
them in a magazine, either, so I know they ain't been published."

"How many pictures were there?"

"About three dozen."

"Sexy?"

"Mister," Blier said softly.

"And Lucy Mitchell came to you today to get those pictures?"

"You could've knocked me over with a ten-ton truck. Man, has she changed. She looked like she just got out of a monastery for women. I told her I ain't got the pictures. She told me I was working in cahoots with a guy named Sy Kramer. I told her she was nuts. I don't know any Kramers except a guy named Dean Kramer who runs one of the girlie books. She wanted to know if this Dean Kramer was related to her Sy Kramer. I told her for all I know he could be related to Martha Kramer for all I know, does she think I'm the Library of Congress?"

"What did she say?"

"She wanted Kramer's name and address. I gave it to her. What I don't understand is this: why, after all these years, she suddenly wants the pictures back? This I don't understand."

"And you don't know anyone named Sy Kramer, is that right?"

"What? Are you starting on me, too?"

"Do you or don't you?"

"I don't. I don't even know *Dean* Kramer so hot. I sold him maybe half a dozen shots since the magazine started. He's a very literary-type guy. He likes literary cheesecake."

"What kind of cheesecake is that?"

"It's got to have a story with it. A beautiful doll ain't enough for Kramer. He needs a story, too. He thinks this way he fools his readers into thinking they ain't looking at a beautiful doll, they're reading maybe *War and Peace,* instead. Man, what a comedown this Lucy Mitchell was today. Why's she wearing that old circus tent? Is she afraid somebody's gonna whistle at her?"

"Maybe she is," Hawes said thoughtfully.

"In the old days . . ." Blier paused, lost in his reminiscence. Then, very softly, almost reverently, he said, "Mister."

Chapter 7

The magazine had a very virile name.

It occurred to Hawes as he stepped into the office that there was not a single virile word in the dictionary that had not been affixed to the front cover of some men's magazine. He wondered when they would begin choosing titles like:

COWARD, the magazine for you and me.

SLOB, for men who don't care.

HE-HE, the magazine of togetherness.

He smiled and entered the reception room. The room was lined with oil paintings of bare-chested men doing various dangerous things, paintings that had undoubtedly been used for magazine covers and then framed and hung. There was a painting of a bare-chested man fighting a shark with a homemade dirk; another of a bare-chested man loading the breech of a cannon; another of a bare-chested man scalping an Indian; another of a bare-chested man in a whip duel with another bare-chested man.

A girl who was almost bare-chested sat behind a desk tucked into one corner of the reception room. Hawes almost fell in love with her, but he controlled himself admirably. The girl looked up from her typing as he approached the desk.

"I'd like to see Dean Kramer," he said. "Police business." He flashed the tin. The girl looked at the shield uninterestedly, and then lazily buzzed Kramer. Hawes was glad he had not fallen in love with her.

"You can go right in, sir. Room Ten in the middle of the hall."

"Thank you," Hawes said. He opened the door leading to the inner offices and started down the hall. The corridor was lined with photographs of old guns, sports cars, and girls in bathing suits—staple items without which any men's magazine would fold instantly. Every men's magazine editor instinctively knew that every man in America was interested in old guns, sports cars, and girls in bathing suits.

Hardly an afternoon went by on patios across the nation when men did not discuss old guns, or sports cars, or girls in bathing suits. Hawes could understand the girls. But the only gun in which he was interested was the one tucked into his shoulder holster. And his concern for the automotive industry centered in the old Ford that took him to work every day.

There was no door on Room Ten. Neither were there true walls to the office. There were, instead, shoulder-high partitions that divided one office from the next. A wide opening in the partition which served as the front wall formed the entrance to the office. Hawes knocked gently on the partition, to the right of the opening. A man inside turned in a swivel chair to face Hawes.

"Mr. Kramer?"

"Yes?"

"Detective Hawes."

"Come in, please," Kramer said. He was an intense little man with bright brown eyes and a sweeping nose. His hair was black and unruly, and he sported a thick black mustache under his nose. The mustache, Hawes figured, had been grown in an attempt to add years to the face. It succeeded only partially; Kramer looked no older than twenty-five. "Sit down, sit down," he said.

Hawes sat in a chair next to his desk. The desk was covered with illustrations for stories, pin-up photos, literary agents' submissions in the variously colored folders that identified their agencies.

Kramer caught Hawes's glance. "A magazine office," he said. "They're all the same. Only the product is different."

Hawes speculated for a moment on the differences between the various products. He remained silent.

"At least," Kramer said, "we try to make our book a little different. It has to be different, or it'll get nosed right off the stands."

"I see," Hawes said.

"What can I do for you, Mr. Hawes? You're not from the postal authorities, are you?"

"No."

"We had a little trouble with one issue we sent through the mails. We thought our permission to mail the book would be lifted. Thank God, it wasn't. And thank God, you're not from the Post Office."

"I'm from the city police," Hawes said.

"What can I do for you, Mr. Hawes?"

"Did a woman named Lucy Mitchell come to see you to-day?"

Kramer looked surprised. "Why, yes. Yes, she did. How did—?"

"What did she want?"

"She thought I might have some pictures belonging to her. I assured her I did not. She also thought I was related to someone she knew."

"Sy Kramer?"

"Yes, that was the name."

"Are you related?"

"No."

"Have you ever seen these pictures of Lucy Mitchell?"

"I see cheesecake all day long, Mr. Hawes. I couldn't know Lucy Mitchell from Margaret Mitchell." He paused, frowned momentarily, and then said, " 'Scarlett O'Hara was not beautiful, but men seldom realized it when caught by her charm as the Tarleton twins were.' "

"What?" Hawes asked.

"The first line of *Gone with the Wind*. It's a hobby of mine. I memorize the opening lines of important novels. The opening line of a book is perhaps the most important line in the book. Did you know that?"

"No, I didn't know that."

"Sure," Kramer said. "That's a theory of mine. You'd be surprised how much authors pack into that first line. It's a very important line."

"About those pictures . . ." Hawes said.

" 'Stately, plump Buck Mulligan came from the stairhead, bearing a bowl of lather on which a mirror and a razor lay crossed,' " Kramer said. "Do you know what that is?"

"No, what is it?"

"*Ulysses*," Kramer said. "James Joyce. It's an example of the naming-the-character school of opening lines. Here's one for you." He paused and got it straight in his mind. " 'It was Wang Lung's wedding day.' "

"*The Good Earth*," Hawes said.

"Yes," Kramer answered, surprised. "How about this one?" Again he thought for a moment. Then he quoted, " 'Whether I shall turn out to be the hero of my own life, or whether that station will be held by anybody else, these pages must show.' "

Hawes was silent.

"It's an old one," Kramer said.

Hawes was still silent.

"David Copperfield," Kramer said.

"Oh, sure," Hawes answered.

"I know thousands of them," Kramer said enthusiastically. "I can reel them—"

"What about those pictures of Lucy Mitchell?"

"What about them?"

"Did she say why she wanted them?"

"She said only that she was sure someone had them. She thought that person might be me. I told her I was not the least bit interested in her *or* her pictures. In short, Mr. Hawes, I played Taps for her." Kramer's face grew brighter. "Here's a dozy," he said. "Listen."

"I'd rather—"

" 'When he finished packing, he walked out on to the third-floor porch of the barracks brushing the dust from his hands, a very neat and deceptively slim young man in the summer khakis that were still early morning fresh.' " Kramer beamed. "Know it?"

"No."

"From Here to Eternity. Jones packs a hell of a lot into that first line. He tells you it's summer, he tells you it's morning, he tells you you're on an Army post with a soldier who is obviously leaving for someplace, and he gives you a thumbnail description of his hero. That's a good opening line."

"Can we get back to Lucy Mitchell?" Hawes said impatiently.

"Certainly," Kramer said, his enthusiasm unabated.

"What did she say about Sy Kramer?"

"She said he had once had the pictures, but she was now certain someone else had them."

"Did she say why she was certain?"

"No."

"And you've never seen these pictures?"

"Mr. Hawes, I veritably cut my way through a cheese-cake jungle every day of the—" Kramer stopped, and his eyes lighted with inner fire. "Here's one!" he said. "Here's one I really enjoy."

"Mr. Kramer . . ." Hawes tried, but Kramer was already gathering steam.

" 'The building presented a not unpleasant architectural

scheme, the banks of wide windows reflecting golden sunlight, the browned weathered brick façade, the ivy clinging
to the brick and framing the windows.' "

"Mr. Kramer . . ."

"That's from *The Bl*—"

"Mr. Kramer!"

"Sir?" Kramer said.

"Is there anything else you can tell me about Lucy
Mitchell?"

"No," Kramer said, seemingly a little miffed.

"Or Sy Kramer?"

"No."

"But she did seem certain that someone else now had
those pictures?"

"Yes, she did."

"Had you ever met her before today?"

"Never."

"Okay," Hawes said. "Thank you very much, Mr. Kramer."

"Not at all," Kramer said. He shook hands with Hawes,
and Hawes rose. "Come again," Kramer said.

And then, as Hawes went through the opening in the
partition, Kramer began quoting, " 'Last night I dreamt I
went to Manderley again. It seemed to me I stood by the
iron gate . . .' "

It seemed to Hawes that several things were obvious at
this stage of the investigation.

To begin with, there was no doubt—and there had never
been any—that Sy Kramer had been extorting five hundred
dollars a month from Lucy Mencken. It was obvious, too,
that Kramer extorted the money on the threat of releasing
the cheesecake photos that had somehow come into his possession. Lucy Mencken had stated that her husband was a
politician who would be running for the state senate in
November. In the hands of the opposing party, or even in
the hands of a newspaper campaigning against Charles
Mencken, the photos could be used with deadly results. It
was understandable why Lucy Mencken wanted to suppress
them. She had come a long way from the farm girl who'd
taken off her clothes for Jason Poole the photographer.
Somewhere along the line, she'd married Charles Mencken,
acquired an exurban estate, and become the mother of two
children. Those pictures could threaten her husband's sena-

torial chances and—if he, too, did not know about them—
could even threaten the smooth fabric of her everyday existence.

There were thirty-six pictures, Patrick Blier had said.

The $500 payment came every month, as did the $300
payment from Edward Schlesser, and the $1,100 payment
from a person or persons unknown. Whenever Schlesser
had delivered his check, Kramer had in turn sent back another photostated copy of the letter. Schlesser had hoped
the photostated copies would eventually run out. Perhaps
he had not realized that it was possible to make a photostat
of a photostat and that Kramer could conceivably have
milked him for the rest of his life. Or perhaps he did realize
it, and simply didn't give a damn. According to what he'd
said, he considered the extortion a bona fide business ex-
pense, like advertising.

But assuming that Kramer had followed a similar *modus
operandi* with Lucy Mencken, could he not have mailed her
a photo and negative each time he received her $500
check? Thirty-six negatives and prints at $500 a throw
amounted to $18,000. It was conceivable that Kramer had
hit upon this easy payment plan simply because $18,000 in
one bite was pretty huge for the average person to swallow.
Especially if that person is trying to keep something secret.
You don't just draw $18,000 from the bank and say you
bought a few new dresses last week.

Then, too—in keeping with Kramer's M.O.—could he
not have been planning on a lifetime income? In the same
way that he could have had a limitless number of copies of
the letter to Schlesser, could he not also have had a limitless
number of glossy prints—all capable of being reproduced
in a newspaper—of the Mencken photos? And could he
not, when the last negative was delivered, then say he had
prints to sell at such and such a price per print?

Had Lucy Mencken realized this?

Had *she* killed Sy Kramer?

Perhaps.

And now there was a new aspect to the case. Lucy
Mencken was certain that someone else had come into possession of the photos. She had undoubtedly learned this
during the past few days, and the first thing she'd done was
to visit Blier and then Kramer, the magazine editor. *Did*
someone now hold those photos, and had this someone con-
tacted Lucy in an attempt to pick up the extortion where it

had ended with Sy Kramer's death? And who was this someone?

And—if Lucy had caused the death of Sy Kramer—could not this new extortionist provoke a second murder?

Hawes nodded reflectively.

It seemed like the time to put a tap on Lucy Mencken's phone.

The man from the telephone company was colored. He showed telephone-company credentials to Lucy Mencken when she opened the door for him. He told her they'd been having some trouble with her line and he might have to make minor repairs.

The man's name was Arthur Brown, and he was a detective attached to the 87th Squad.

He put bugs on the three telephones in the house, carrying his lines across the back of the Mencken property, where they crossed the road and fed into a recorder in a supposed telephone-company shack on the other side of the road. The machine would begin recording automatically whenever any of the phones was lifted from its cradle. The machine would record incoming calls and outgoing calls indiscriminately. Calls to the butcher, calls from relatives and friends, angry calls, personal calls—all would be recorded faithfully and later listened to in the squadroom. None of the recorded information would be admissible as court evidence.

But some of it might lead to the person or persons who were threatening Lucy Mencken anew.

Chapter 8

When Mario Torr stopped by at the squadroom, Bert Kling was on the phone talking to his fiancée. Torr waited outside the railing until Kling was finished talking. He looked at Kling expectantly, and Kling motioned him to enter. As before, Torr was dressed in immaculate mediocrity. He went to the chair beside Kling's desk and sat in it, carefully preserving the crease in his trousers.

"I just thought I'd stop by to see how things were going along," he said.

"Things are going along fine," Kling said.

"Any leads?"

"A few."

"Good," Torr said. "Sy was my friend. I'd like to see justice done. Do you still think this was a gang rumble?"

"We're working on a few possibilities," Kling said.

"Good," Torr answered.

"Why didn't you tell me you'd taken a fall, Torr?"

"Huh?"

"One-to-two at Castleview for extortion. You did a year's time and were paroled. How about it, Torr?"

"Oh, yeah," Torr said. "It must've slipped my mind."

"Sure."

"I'm straight now," Torr said. "I got a good job, been at it since I got out."

"Sand's Spit, right?"

"Right. I'm a laborer. I make about ninety bucks a week. That's pretty good money."

"I'm glad," Kling said.

"Sure. There's no percentage in crime."

"Or in bad associates," Kling said.

"Huh?"

"A man going straight shouldn't have had a friend like Sy Kramer."

"That was strictly social. Look, I believe a guy's business

62

is his own business. I don't like to mess. He never talked about his business, and I never talked about mine."

"But you figured he was working something, right?"

"Well, he always dressed nice and drove a fancy car. Sure, I figured he was working something."

"Did you ever meet his floozy?"

"Nancy O'Hara? Mr. Kling, that ain't a floozy. If you ever met her, you wouldn't call her no floozy. Far from it."

"Then you did meet her?"

"Once. Sy was drivin' by with her in the Caddy. I waved to him, and he stopped to say hello. He introduced her."

"She claims she knew nothing about his business. Do you buy that, Torr?"

"I buy it. Who says a woman needs brains? All the brains she needs is right between—"

"That makes two of you who didn't know anything about Sy's business."

"I figured he had something big going for him," Torr said. "He had to. A guy don't come into a couple of cars and a new pad and clothes to knock your eyes out unless he's got something big going for him. I don't mean penny-ante stuff, either. I mean *big*."

"What do you consider penny-ante?"

"Pin money. You know."

"No, I don't. What's pin money?"

"A couple of bills a month, you know. Hell, you can tell me better than I can tell you. How much was he getting from his marks?"

"Enough," Kling said.

"I don't mean the big marks, I mean the small ones," Torr said.

"How do you know there are big ones and small ones?"

"I'm just guessing," Torr said. "I figure the big ones set him up with the cars and the pad. The small ones buy his bread. Ain't I right?"

"You could be."

"Sure. So what can you expect from a small mark? Two, three bills? Five grand in a lump? It's the big ones that count."

"I guess so," Kling said.

"Do you know who the ones are yet?"

"No."

"The small ones?"

"Maybe."

"How many small ones are there?"

"You should have been a cop, Torr."

"I'm only interested in seeing justice done. Sy was my friend."

"Justice will triumph," Kling said. "I'm busy. If you're finished, I'd like to get back to work."

"Sure," Torr said. "I didn't mean to disturb you."

And he left.

The call from Danny Gimp had told Carella that the informer had something for him, could they meet someplace away from the precinct? It had been Carella's policy—up to the day of his idiocy—to give his home-phone number to no one but relatives, close friends, and of course the desk sergeant. He did not encourage business calls at home. It was annoying enough to be called there by the squad; he did not want crime detection or law enforcement to intrude on his off-duty hours. He had broken this rule with Danny Gimp.

The working arrangement between a cop and a stool pigeon is—even with men who bear no particular fondness for each other—a highly personal one. Crime detection is a great big horse race, and you choose your jockeys carefully. And a jockey working for your stable does not report your horse's morning running-time to the owner of a rival stable. The bulls of the 87th worked with various stoolies, and these stoolies reported to them faithfully. The transaction was a business one, pure and simple—information for money. But a certain amount of trust and faith was involved. The policeman trusted the stoolie's information and was willing to pay for it. The stoolie trusted the policeman to pay him once the information had been divulged. Cops were averse to working with pigeons they did not know and trust. And likewise, pigeons—whose sole source of income was the information they garnered here and there—were not overly fond of displaying their wares before a strange cop.

A call from the stoolie to the squad was generally a call directed at one cop and one cop alone. If that cop was off-duty or otherwise out of the office, the stoolie would not speak to anyone else, thanks. He would wait. Waiting could sometimes result in a lost collar. Waiting, in a homicide case, could sometimes result in another homicide. And so Danny Gimp had Carella's home-phone number, and it was there that he called him when the desk sergeant informed him Carella was off that day.

The men arranged to meet at Plum Beach in Riverhead. Carella told Danny to bring along his swimming trunks.

They lay side by side on the sand like two old cronies who were discussing the bathing beauties. The sun was very strong that day.

"I hope you don't mind my not wanting to come to the precinct," Danny said. "I don't like to be seen there too often. It hurts my business."

"I understand," Carella said. "What have you got for me?"

"The background on Sy Kramer."

"Go ahead."

"He's been living big for a few years, Steve, but not as big as just before he got it. You know, he had a nice pad and a good car—a Dodge—but nothing like the new joint, and nothing like the Caddy, you dig?"

"I dig."

A boy ran by, kicking sand in Carella's face.

"I used to be a ninety-seven-pound weakling," Carella said, and Danny grinned.

"Okay," Danny said. "In September, he goes berserk. Spends like a drunken sailor. Two new cars, clothes, the new pad. This is when he picks up the O'Hara bitch. She's impressed by loot, what dame isn't? She moves in with him."

"How'd he meet her?"

"How'd she say?"

"She said she's a dancer, met him in a drugstore."

"For the birds," Danny said. "She did a crumby strip in a joint on The Stem. Half her salary came from conning guys into buying her colored water."

"Prostitution?"

"Not from what I could gather, but I wouldn't put it past her. She's quite a looker, Steve. They billed her as Red Garters."

"That's a name for a stripper, all right."

"Well, she's got this flaming-red hair. Anyway, her act stunk. All she had was a body. The less dancing she did, the quicker she got her clothes off, the better it was for everybody concerned."

"So she met Kramer and latched onto him," Carella said.

"Right. I think she read the writing on the wall. She was

getting pawed by a hundred strangers a night for peanuts. She figured she might as well get pawed by only one guy, and live in luxury."

"You're a cynic, Danny," Carella said.

"I read the cards," Danny said, shrugging. "Anyway, Kramer hit it big in September."

"How?"

"That's the one thing I don't know."

"Mmm," Carella said.

"I take it you know all this already? I ain't giving you nothing new."

"Most of it," Carella said. "I didn't know about the girl. What else have you got?"

"A hunting trip."

"Kramer?"

"Yes."

"When?"

"Beginning of September. It was after he come back that he started throwing the green around. Think there's a tie-in?"

"I don't know. Has he got a rep as a hunter?"

"Rabbits, birds, stuff like that. He's never shot a tiger, if that's what you mean."

"Where'd he go on this trip?"

"I don't know."

"Did he go alone?"

"Yes."

"Are you sure it was a hunting trip?"

"Nope. It could have been anything. For all I know, he could have gone to Chicago and rubbed somebody. Maybe that's where he got the lump of dough."

"Did he come back with the money?"

"No. Unless he was real cool with it and didn't start flashing it around. The trip was in the beginning of the month. He didn't start spending until the end of the month."

"Was the money hot, do you suppose?"

"Not the way he spent it, Steve. If it was hot, he'd have used a money changer and taken a loss."

"How do you know he didn't?"

"I checked the guys buying hot bills. Kramer didn't go to see any of them. Besides, we're forgetting something."

"What?"

"His racket. He's an extortionist. True, he may have decided to do a quick rub job for somebody, but you don't hire a shakedown artist for a torpedo job. Besides, like I told you, this torpedo crap went out in the—"

"Mmm, maybe you're right," Carella said. "But he could have carried hot ice or furs—"

"He ain't a fence, Steve. He's a shakedown artist."

"Still."

"I don't buy it. Maybe this hunting trip was a cover. Maybe he went to see a mark." Danny shrugged. "Wherever he went, it netted him a big pile of bills."

"Maybe he really *did* go on a hunting trip," Carella said. "Maybe the trip and the dough have no connection."

"Maybe," Danny said.

"But you don't know where he went, is that right?"

"Not a glimmer."

"And he went alone?"

"Right."

"Was this before he met the O'Hara girl?"

"Yes."

"Think she might know something about it?"

"Maybe." Danny smiled. "Guys have been known to talk in their sleep."

"We'll check her again. You've helped, Danny. How much?"

"I don't like to hit you too hard, Steve. Especially when I didn't give you so much. But I'm slightly from Brokesville. Can you spare a quarter of a century?"

Carella reached for his wallet and gave danny two tens and a five.

"Thanks," Danny said. "I'll make it up to you. The next one's on the house."

They lay on the sand for a little while longer. Carella went into the water for a quick dip, and then they went back to the locker rooms. They shook hands, and left each other at three in the afternoon.

Love, fleeting chimera that it is, was hardly present at all the second time Cotton Hawes called upon Nancy O'Hara. In fact, aside from their use of first names in addressing each other, one hardly could have guessed they'd shared the most intimate of intimacies. Ah, love. Easy come, easy go.

"Hello, Nancy," he said when she opened the door. "I .hope I didn't catch you at a bad time."

"No," she said. "Come in, Cotton."

He followed her into the living room.

"Drink?"

"No. Thanks."

"What is it, Cotton? Have you found the murderer?"

"Not yet. A few more questions, if you don't mind."

"Not at all."

"Were you a stripper?"

Nancy hesitated. "Yes."

"Anything else?"

"No."

"Okay."

"Thanks. I'm glad I have your seal of approval."

"Why'd you lie?"

"A dancer sounds better than a stripper. I'm a lousy dancer, and a worse stripper. Sy wanted me to live with him. So I lived with him. Is there something so terrible about that?"

"I guess not."

"Don't get moral, Cotton," she told him. "You weren't very goddamn moral in bed."

"True." He grinned. "End of sermon. End of shocked Daughter of American Revolution routine. Beginning of important questions."

"Like what?"

"Like Kramer. Did he ever mention a hunting trip to you?"

"Yes." She paused. "I told you. Hunting was one of his hobbies."

"A hunting trip in September?"

"Yes." Again, she paused. "Before we met. Yes, he mentioned it."

"Did he really go hunting?"

"I think so. He talked about the stuff he'd shot. A deer, I think. Yes, he really went hunting."

"Where?"

"I don't know."

"Did he go hunting again while you were living with him?"

"Yes. I already told you this. He went several times."

"But you don't know where he went that time in September?"

"No."

Hawes thought for a moment. Then he said, "Would you happen to know if Kramer had a gasoline credit card?"

"A what?"

"A credit card. To show at service stations. So that he could charge his gas."

"Oh. I don't know. Would he carry that with him?"

"Yes."

"Well, the police still have his wallet. Why not look through it?"

"We will," Hawes said. "Did Kramer save bills?"

"You mean grocery bills and things like that?"

"No. I mean telephone bills, electric-light bills, gasoline bills. Things like that."

"Yes. Why, yes, he did."

"Where did he keep them?"

"In the desk in the foyer."

"Would they still be there?"

"I haven't touched anything," Nancy said.

"Good. Mind if I look through the desk?"

"Not at all. What are you looking for, Cotton?"

"Something that might be just as good as a road map," he answered, and he went out to the foyer and the desk.

Chapter 9

Sy Kramer had a card with the Meridian Mobilube Company that enabled him to charge his automobile expenses at any of their gasoline stations. Most of the bills in his desk for gasoline charges had been signed at a place called George's Service Center in Isola. George's, the police discovered after a check of the phone book, was a station three blocks from Kramer's apartment. He had undoubtedly been a regular customer there and most of his gas purchases had originated there. The bills he had signed looked like this:

On September first, Kramer had started a trip. The first bill for that date came from George's, in Isola. Kramer had put thirteen gallons of gasoline and a quart of oil into the car. A check with the manufacturer of Kramer's 1952-model automobile revealed that the tank capacity of the car was seventeen gallons, and that the car could be expected to travel between fifteen and sixteen miles on a gallon of gasoline. The bills Sy Kramer signed that day seemed to back up the manufacturer's word. Kramer had apparently kept a careful eye on his tank gauge. Approximately every hundred miles, when the gauge registered half-empty, he had stopped and brought it up to *full* again, signing a credit slip for the gas. Each bill was stamped with the name of the gas station and the town.

Sy Kramer had unmistakably gone to the Adirondack Mountains in New York State.

Using a road map, Hawes traced Kramer's progression across that state, marking each town for which he had a bill. The last place in which Kramer had stopped for gas on September first was called Gloversville. From that town, the mountain territory spread north. From that town, he could have gone anywhere in the Adirondacks; he had not signed another bill for gasoline that day. Hawes marked Gloversville with a big circle, and then he consulted the bills once more.

CO 92 (7.56)

This charge and any refund of taxes due dealer are assigned to:

MERIDIAN MOBILUBE COMPANY, INC.

06967   DATE __6/12__ 19 __57__

PRINT   CUSTOMER'S NAME

MR. S. KRAMER

CITY **ISOLA**   STATE

CREDIT CARD NUMBER   LICENSE NO.

133 - 397 - 066

RECEIVED PRODUCTS AND QUANTITIES SPECIFIED BELOW:

CUSTOMER'S SIGNATURE X *Seymour Kramer*

QUANTITY	PRODUCT OR SERVICE	MEMO TAXES FED.	STATE	UNIT PRICE	AMOUNT
16⁺ GALS.	MERIDIAN REGULAR GAS				5 84
"	MERIDIAN HI-TEST GAS				
"					
1 QTS.	MERIDIAN OIL				45
"	MERIDIAN SPECIAL OIL				
"	MOTOR OIL				
	LUBRICATION				

CUSTOMER'S COPY

All Applicable Taxes Are Included Hereon

SALES TAX	02
TOTAL	6 31

George's Svce Center

Isola

DEALER'S NAME, ADDRESS, CITY AND STATE ☐

On September eighth, a week later, Kramer had put five
gallons of gasoline and a quart of oil into the car. He had
made the purchase in a town called Griffins. The rest of the
bills for September eighth recorded a southbound trip that
eventually led back to the city. The stop in Griffins had apparently been the first stop for gas on the leg home. The
town north of Griffins was Bakers Mills. It seemed possible
to Hawes that Kramer had gone into the mountains somewhere between Griffins and Bakers Mills. He circled both
towns. It seemed likely, too, that Griffins had been the first
town he'd hit after coming out of the mountains, gassing up
there for the first lap of the trip home.

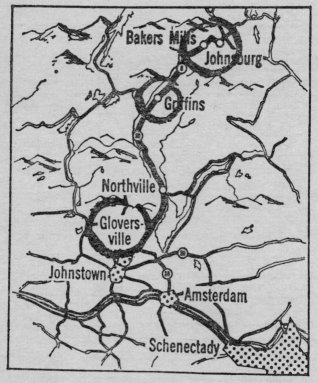

His calculations could, he admitted, be wrong. But the
distance from Gloversville to Griffins was an approximate

thirty-five miles. Kramer had filled his tank in Gloversville. Figuring fifteen miles to the gallon, Kramer would have used a little more than two gallons to make the trip from Gloversville to Griffins. Could Hawes safely assume Kramer had then traveled another approximate fifteen miles into the mountains, and an additional fifteen miles for the return trip to Griffins, where he had added five gallons of gas to the tank?

It was possible that Griffins had been his springboard into the mountains. It was a long shot, but it was possible.

One thing was certain. Kramer was either a liar or a habitual lawbreaker. He had told Nancy O'Hara he'd shot a deer.

A check with one of the state's game protectors revealed that the Adirondack deer season did not start until October twenty-fifth.

"Hello, Jean?"

"Yes?"

"This is Lucy Mencken."

"Oh, hello, Lucy, how are you? I was just thinking about you."

"Really?"

"I was going to call you for that stuffed-pepper recipe. The one you used for the last buffet."

"Oh, that. Did you really like them that much?"

"Lucy, they were magnificent!"

"I'm glad. I'll bring you the recipe . . . or perhaps . . . well, the reason I'm calling, Jean, I thought you and the children might like to come over for a swim this afternoon. The water's just grand, and it looks as if it's going to be a terribly hot day."

"Yes, it does. I don't know, Lucy. Frank said he might be home early . . ."

"Well, bring him along. Charles is here."

"He is?"

"Yes. Jean, you know you have a standing invitation to swim here whenever you like. I feel awfully silly having to call to invite you each time."

"Well . . ."

"Say you'll come."

"What time, Lucy?"

"Whenever you like. Come for lunch, if you can."

"All right, I'll be there."

"Good. I'll be waiting for you."

The recorder in the mock telephone-company shack across the highway wound its tapes relentlessly. Arthur Brown, monitoring the calls, was bored to tears. He had brought along a dozen back issues of *National Geographic*, and he read those now while Lucy and her various contacts talked and talked and talked. Thus far, there had been no threatening calls.

But the telephone of Lucy Mencken was damned busy.

The telephone of Teddy Carella was not busy at all. To Teddy Carella, the telephone was a worthless instrument designed for people who, in one respect alone, were more fortunate than she.

Teddy Carella was a deaf-mute.

Her handicap had been an unfortunate accident of birth, but she was more fortunate than other women in many other respects, and so she never gave much thought to it. Her greatest fortune was her husband, Steve Carella. She would never tire of looking at him, never tire of "listening" to him, never tire of loving him.

On the evening of July eighth, after dinner, she and Carella were sitting in the living room of their Riverhead apartment watching television. Reading the lips of the performers, Teddy glanced at Carella and realized that she was watching television alone. Her husband was up somewhere on cloud thirteen. She smiled. Her entire face seemed to open when she smiled. Dark-haired, dark-eyed, she embodied the physical attributes of a Venus, which were somehow combined with the impishness of a Puck. Wearing a skirt and halter, she came up out of her chair, went to sit at Carella's feet, and then gestured with her head toward the television screen, her black eyebrows raised questioningly.

"Huh?" Carella said. "Oh, it's a good show. Wonderful, wonderful."

Teddy nodded, burlesquing the expression on his face.

"Really," Carella said sincerely. "I love summer-replacement shows. They've got a lot of spark, a lot of imagination. Wonderful, wonderful."

She gazed at him steadily.

"Okay," he admitted, "I was thinking about the case."

Teddy moved her mouth slightly and then pointed to herself.

"I'll tell you about it, if you really want to hear it," he said.

She nodded.

"Well, Hawes is working on it with me."

Teddy pulled a sour face.

"No, no," Carella said, "he's going to be all right. He's going to be a good man." He grinned. "Remember. You heard it here first."

Teddy grinned back.

"I told you about the kill, and the bank accounts, and about Kramer's victims. We still haven't located the eleven-hundred-dollar mark, and Lucy Mencken still seems like our best bet for the grand award. But a couple of things keep bothering me."

Teddy nodded, listening intently.

"Well, for one thing, where did Kramer keep these extortion documents? The photostated copies of the letter, the pictures of Lucy, and whatever he had on this eleven-hundred-dollar mark. Not to mention the big babies in the bank book. We went over his apartment with a fine comb, but there wasn't anything there. Hey, honey, you should see this redhead he was shacking with. Now, that's my idea of a woman."

Teddy frowned menacingly.

"Very pretty," Carella said. "Very pretty. I think I'll go back there and make another search for important documents. I think he might have kept them in the bedroom, don't you?"

Teddy nodded her head in an exaggerated, *"Sure* he did!"

"Seriously, honey, it bothers me. You'd figure a safety deposit box, wouldn't you?"

Again, Teddy nodded.

"Well, I put a check on all the banks in the city. No safety deposit boxes for Sy or Seymour Kramer. I got a list of eighty-five S. K. box holders—people with the initials S. K., you understand. Just in case Kramer used a phony name for the box. When a guy picks a phony, he'll sometimes use his own initials. We called each and every one of those names. They're all legitimate. So where the hell did Kramer hide the documents?"

Teddy licked an imaginary letter with her tongue.

"A post office box?" Carella asked. "Possibly. We checked his local post office, and he didn't have one there.

But it could be anyplace in the city. I'll have a check started in the morning. But I don't think we'll turn up anything. We didn't find any unexplained keys in his effects."

Teddy turned an imaginary knob.

"That's right," he said, "some post offices have those little combination knobs on their boxes. It's a possibility, all right." He kissed her rapidly. "You're a helpmeet indeed."

She was in the process of getting set to kiss him more soundly, when he began shaking his head morosely.

What is it? her eyes asked.

"The other thing that bothers me is that bankbook," he said. "Now, what the hell kind of extortion money is that? The only sensible entry is the fifteen thousand dollars. But if you were extorting money from me, would you come and ask for six thousand three hundred and twenty dollars and fourteen cents?"

Teddy looked puzzled.

"No, honey, that wasn't an actual entry," he explained. "I'm just trying to make a point. Why should Kramer have asked for twenty-*one* thousand dollars? Isn't that a crazy figure? Wouldn't *twenty* thousand be a more likely figure, assuming you were just picking figures out of the hat? And why *nine* thousand? Wouldn't *ten* be more likely? I don't get it. I always thought people preferred nice fat round figures."

Teddy began writing on the air. It took Carella a moment to realize she was doing imaginary addition.

"Sure, sure," he said. "Twenty-one thousand and nine thousand equal thirty thousand—and that's a nice round figure. You think maybe he asked his victim for it in two lumps?"

Teddy nodded.

"Then what about the third lump? And why weren't the first and second lumps in even figures? There's something funny about it, Teddy. And I keep thinking if we can find Kramer's bunk, find his goddamn hiding place, we'll learn a lot about those figures. Those are the biggest deposits he made, honey. We're chasing around after the small potatoes, and we haven't even an inkling to the identity of the big one—the one who *could* have committed murder. Oh, what the hell, I guess Lucy Mencken could have done it, too. She's been chasing around like a wild woman looking for those pictures of hers. I'd like to get a look at them. I'd like to see her without her space suit."

Again Teddy frowned.

"You know I love you dearly," Carella said, grinning. "You're a wonderful kid." He paused. "I love you, kid—but, oh, that Mencken's wife."

Teddy tried a frown and then burst out laughing. She flung herself into his arms, and he said, "Hey, hey, how'm I ever gonna solve this case if you carry on like that?"

But he had already stopped thinking about the case.

Oh, that Cotton Hawes.

On Tuesday morning, July ninth, he left the city.

It was truly a beautiful day, not too hot for July, but with the sun shining brightly overhead and a fresh breeze blowing in over the River Harb. He crossed the Hamilton Bridge, at the foot of which a dead blond girl had been found long before Hawes had been transferred to the 87th. The River Harb looked quiet and still that day. He went into the next state, following the Greentree Highway, which bounded the river, heading north. He drove with the top of his Ford down. His jacket rested on the seat beside him. He wore a sports shirt with wide alternating black and red stripes. He wore old Navy gray trousers. Hawes had once been a chief petty officer, and he still had most of his Navy clothes. He wore them often, not because of sentiment but simply because his cop's salary didn't allow the range to buy all the clothes he'd have liked to own.

The wind caught at his red hair as he drove along. The sun beat down on his head and shoulders. It was a good day, and he was beginning to feel in a slightly holiday mood, almost forgetting why he was driving to upstate New York. He remembered again when he passed Castleview Prison. He could look across the River Harb into his own state, and there he could see the gray walls of the prison merging with the sheer face of the cliff that dropped to the river's edge below. Directly opposite, almost on the road he drove, was the castle from which the prison derived its name. The castle had allegedly been built by a Dutch patroom in the days of early settlement. It stared across the river and into the next state, providing an excellent view of the prison walls. And from the prison, the castle could be seen, and so it was called Castleview. He looked at the prison now with only passing interest. It would one day, in the not too distant future, become an integral part of his life, but he did not know that now, and he would not know it until long after the Kramer case had been solved.

On that July morning it only reminded him of crime and punishment, and it brought his thoughts back to the reason for his trip to the Adirondacks. When he stopped for lunch that afternoon, his mind began to wander because, alas, he fell in love.

The girl with whom he fell in love was a waitress.

She wore a white dress and a white cap on her clipped blond hair. She came to his table, and she smiled, and the smile knocked him clear back against the wall.

"Good afternoon, sir," she said. When he heard her voice, he was hopelessly gone. "Would you care to see a menu?"

"I have a better idea," Hawes said.

"What's that?"

"Go back and change into your street clothes. Show me the best restaurant in town, and I'll buy you lunch there."

The girl looked at him with a half-amused, half-shocked expression on her face. "I've heard of speed demons," she said, "but you just broke the sound barrier."

"Life is sweet and short," Hawes said.

"And you're getting old," the girl replied. "Even your hair's turning white."

"What do you say?"

"I say I don't even know your name. I say I couldn't possibly have lunch with you because I don't get off until I'm relieved at four. I also say you're from the city."

"I am." Hawes paused. "How'd you know?"

"I'm from the city myself. Majesta."

"That's a nice section."

"It's fine. Especially when you compare it to this hick village."

"You here for the summer?"

"Yes. I'm going back to college in the fall. I'm a senior."

"Have lunch with me," Hawes said.

"What's your name?"

"Cotton."

"Your first name, I mean."

"That's it."

The girl grinned. "Like Cotton Mather?"

"Exactly. Only it's Cotton Hawes."

"I've never had lunch with a man named Cotton," the girl said.

"Go tell your boss you have a terrible headache. I'm the only customer in the place, anyway. He won't miss either of us."

The girl considered this a moment. "Then what'll I do the rest of the afternoon?" she asked. "Working helps me kill the time. You can go crazy in this miserable village."

Hawes smiled. "We'll figure something out," he said.

The girl's name was Polly. She was an anthropology major, and she hoped to go on for her master's after graduation and then for her doctorate. She wanted to go to Yucatán, she said, to study the Mayan Indians and learn all about the feathered serpent. Hawes learned all this during lunch. She had taken him to a restaurant in the next town, a restaurant that jutted out over a pine-shrouded lake, cantilevering over the waters below. When he told Polly he was a cop, she didn't believe him, and so he showed her his gun. Polly's blue eyes opened wide. Her wonderful mouth curved into a long O. She was a deceptively slender girl with a well-rounded bosom and wide hips. She walked with the angular sveltness of a model.

When they finished lunch, there wasn't much to do in town, and so they had a couple of drinks. The couple of drinks weren't sufficient on a day that was turning hot, and so they had several more. There was a juke box in the lounge off the restaurant, and so they danced. The afternoon was still very young and a good movie was playing in the local theater, and so they went to see it. And then, because it was time for dinner when they once more came into the daylight, they ate again.

There was a long evening ahead.

Polly lived in a two-room cottage near the restaurant for which she worked. The cottage had a record player and whisky, and so they went there after dinner.

Polly lived alone in the cottage. Polly was a very pretty blond girl with blue eyes, deceptively slender with a well-rounded bosom and wide hips. Polly was an anthropology major who wanted to go to Yucatán. Polly was a city girl who was bored to tears with the village and tickled to death she had met this entertaining stranger with a white streak in his hair and a name like Cotton.

She fell in love with him a little bit, too.

She lived alone in the cottage.

And so to bed.

Chapter 10

From the shores of the lake and the entrance to Kukabonga Lodge, you could see the green-backed humps of the
mountains and the clear blue of the sky beyond. The lodge
was small, built of logs that seemed a part of the surround-
ing greenery. A double flight of wooden steps rose from the
flat rock almost at the lake's edge, rose in tentlike ascent to
the front door of the lodge. The front door was a Dutch
door, the top half open now as Hawes mounted the stairs.
He mounted the stairs wearily and almost dejectedly. He
had already checked half a dozen of the lodges scattered
through the mountains, doggedly working his way north
with Griffins as his starting point. None of the lodge owners
remembered a man named Sy Kramer. Most of them admitted that the real hunters didn't come up until the end of
October, when the deer season started. September wasn't
such a good time. One lodge owner admitted his place was
full of what he called "cheater hunters" during the early
part of September. These, he said, were men who came up
with girls after telling their wives they were off to the wilds
to hunt.

Hawes was disappointed. The country was lovely, but he
had not come up here to admire the scenery. Besides, he
was no longer in love and he was becoming rather bored
with the continuous slope of the land, the brazen cloudless
blue of the sky, the constant chatter of birds and insects.
He almost wished he were back in the 87th, where a man
couldn't see the sky for the tenements.

It grows on you, he thought. *It's a hairy bastard, but you
get to love it.*

"Hello, there," a voice at the top of the steps said.

Hawes looked up. "Hello," he said.

The man was standing just behind the lower half of the
Dutch door. The visible half of his body was lean and tight,
the body of an Indian scout, the body of a man who la-
bored in the sun. The man wore a white tee shirt, which

covered the hardness of his muscles like a thin layer of oil.
His face was square and angular; it could have been chiseled from the rock that formed a backdrop for the lodge.
His eyes were blue and piercing. He smoked a pipe leisure-
ly, and the ease with which he smoked softened the first impression of hard muscularity. His voice, too, in contrast to
the wiriness of his body, was soft and gentle, with a mild
twang.

"Welcome to Kukabonga," the man said. "I'm Jerry
Fielding."

"I'm Cotton Hawes. How do you do?"

Fielding opened the lower half of the door and stepped
onto the landing, extending a browned hand. "Glad to
—know you," he said, and they shook. Fielding's eyes darted
to the white streak in Hawes's otherwise red hair. "That a
lightning burn?" he asked.

"No," Hawes said. "I was knifed. The hair grew in
white."

Fielding nodded. "Fellow up here got hit by lightning.
Like Ahab. He's got a streak something like that. How'd
you get knifed?"

"I'm a cop," Hawes said. He was reaching into his back
pocket for identification when Fielding stopped him.

"You don't need it," he said. "I spotted the shoulder
holster when you were bending as you came up the steps."

Hawes smiled. "We can use a man like you," he said.
"Come on down to the city."

"I like it up here," Fielding said graciously. "Who you
chasing, Mr. Hawes?"

"A ghost," Hawes said.

"Not likely to find many of those around here. Come on
inside. I've been hankering for a drink, and I hate like hell
to drink alone. Or aren't you a drinking man?"

"I can use one," Hawes said.

"Of course," Fielding said, as they went into the cabin
together, "I know cops aren't allowed to drink on duty—
but I'm not likely to write a letter to the commissioner. Are
you?"

"I hardly ever write letters to the commissioner," Hawes
said.

"Didn't think you did," Fielding answered.

They were inside the lodge now. A huge stone fireplace
dominated the room. Flanking the fireplace, in the same
pattern as the steps outside, was another double set of stairs

leading, apparently, to rooms just below the peak of the roof. There were four doorways off the main room. One of them was open, and Hawes could see through it into a kitchen.

"What'll it be?" Fielding asked.

"Scotch neat."

"I like a man who drinks his whisky neat," Fielding said, grinning. "It tells me he likes his coffee strong and his women soft. Am I right?"

"You're right," Hawes said.

"Tell you something else about yourself, Mr. Hawes," Fielding said. "I'll bet you've never put a bullet in an animal or a hook in a fish unless you were hungry."

"That's true," Hawes said.

"Ever shot a man?"

"No."

"Not even in the line of duty?"

"No."

"Were you in the service?"

"Yes."

"See action?"

"Yes."

"And you never shot anyone?"

"I was in the Navy," Hawes said.

"What rank?"

"Chief petty officer."

"Doing what?"

"Torpedoes," Hawes said.

"On what?"

"A P.T. boat."

"Chief petty officer on a P.T. boat?" Fielding asked. "You were practically second in command, weren't you?"

"Practically," Hawes said. "The skipper was a j.g. Were you in the Navy?"

"No, but my dad was. He talked about it a lot. He was a regular Navy man, you know. A commander when he died. He's the one built this lodge. He used to come up here whenever he had leave. He loved the place. I guess I do, too." Fielding paused reflectively. "Dad died in Norfolk, behind a desk. I guess he'd have liked to die one of two places. Either on a ship, or here at the lodge. But he died in Norfolk, behind a desk." Fielding shook his head.

"You own the lodge now, Mr. Fielding?" Hawes asked.

"Yes."

"I guess I came to the wrong place," Hawes said.

Fielding looked up. He had poured the whisky, and he brought it to Hawes and then said, "How do you mean?"

"I didn't realize it was a private lodge. I thought you took guests."

"I do. Five at a time. It's my living. I guess I'm what you'd call a bum."

"But you don't have any guests now?"

"Nope. All alone this week. I'm mighty glad to see you."

"Are you open all year round?"

"All year round," Fielding said. "Cheers."

"Drink hearty."

They drank.

"Were you open around September first of last year?" Tawes asked.

"Yep. Had a full house."

Hawes put down the shot glass. "Was one of your guests a man named Sy Kramer?"

"Yep."

"Did he do any hunting?"

"He sure did. Out every day. Brought back all kinds of stuff."

"Deer?"

"No, the deer season doesn't start until October. But he got crows and vermin—and I think he got a red fox."

"Did he spend a lot of money while he was here, Mr. Fielding?"

"On what?" Fielding asked. "Nothing to spend money on in the mountains."

"Was he carrying a lot of cash?"

"If he was, he didn't say anything about it to me."

"Did he come up alone?"

"Yep. I sometimes get them in pairs or in threes, or sometimes a party of five rents the whole lodge. This isn't a whorehouse, Mr. Hawes. I only take men who want to hunt . . . or fish. I've got my own cabin back of the lodge. I entertain girls there frequently . . . but that's private enterprise. I'm intruding on nobody's morals but my own. Any man is free to do whatever the hell he wants to, I figure, but if he comes to my lodge, he comes to hunt or fish. He can screw around on his own time."

"Kramer came up alone, then?"

"They *all* did that trip. Isn't very often that happens, but this time it did. Not one of the five knew each other before they got here."

"You had five guests the week Kramer was here?"

"Yep, and all from the city. Now, wait a minute, wait a minute. One of them checked in on a Wednesday, and he left before the others. He was a good hunter, that one. Fellow named Phil Kettering. Hated to leave. I remember on the Wednesday he checked out, he got up real early in the morning, went off into the woods to hunt a little before he started the trip home. Paid me, took all his bags with him, said he wouldn't be back for lunch, but he just had to get in a little more hunting before driving back. A good hunter, that one."

"How about the others?"

"Kramer was so-so. The other three . . ." Fielding rolled his eyes skyward.

"No good?"

"Bunglers. You know. Tripped over their own feet. I guess they were all amateurs."

"Young men?"

"Two of them were. Let me see if I can remember their names. One of them had a real queer name, foreign sounding. Just give me a minute. . . . Do you want another drink?"

"Thanks, no," Hawes said.

"Will you be staying for dinner?"

"I don't think so. Thanks a lot."

"Be a pleasure to have you."

"I really have to get back to the city. I'm overdue now."

"Well, if you want to stay, speak up. Won't be any trouble at all. Gets lonely as hell here when the house is empty. Now, let me see. This fellow's name. José? Was that it? Something Spanish like that . . . but not his second name. That was hundred-per-cent pure white American Protestant. Joaquim! That was it. Joaquim. That's the way it's pronounced, even though you spell it with a J. Ho-ah-keem. Joaquim Miller, that was it. Some combination, huh?"

"He was one of the young ones, is that right?"

"In his thirties. Married fellow. An electrical engineer, I think. Or an electronics engineer, one of the two. His wife had gone to California to visit her mother, who he didn't get along with. So he came up here to hunt. God, he should have stayed in the city. I don't think he liked the hunting at all. Didn't get a damn thing but a cold in his head."

"How about the others?"

"The other young fellow was about forty, forty-two, pretty well-fixed. Partner in an advertising firm, I think. I got the feeling his wife and him were headed for the divorce courts. I think his getting away from her for a week was a sort of a trial separation. That was the feeling I got, anyway."

"What was his name?"

"Frank . . . something. Just a minute. Frank . . . Reuther, Ruther, that was it. Without an E. Just Ruther. That was his name."

"And the old man? What about him?"

"Sixtyish. Tired businessman. Got the feeling he'd tried everything from skiing to water polo. This was his week to try hunting. It was quite a week, I'm telling you."

"How do you mean?"

"Oh, nothing, except that Kettering got a little bored with the beginners' talk, that's all. He and Kramer hit it off pretty well because he had some inkling of what it was all about. These other fellows, well. Not that they couldn't shoot. They could shoot, all right. Any damn fool can hit a tin can on a back fence. But shooting and hunting are two different things. These men just weren't hunters."

"Was there any trouble that week?"

"How do you mean, trouble?"

"Any fights? Arguments?"

"Yes. One. Kramer got into a little tiff with one of the fellows."

"Which one?" Hawes asked, moving quickly to the edge of his seat.

"Frank Ruther. The advertising man."

"What was the argument about?"

"Clams."

"What?"

"Clams. Kramer was talking about how good steamed clams were. Ruther told him to please change the subject because it made him ill just to think about clams. We were all at the dinner table, you see. Well, Kramer wouldn't change the subject. He began telling about how to prepare them, and how to serve them, and I guess Ruther got a little sick."

"What happened?"

"He got up and yelled, 'Will you shut your goddamn mouth?' He was a little touchy to begin with, you understand. Either that divorce theory of mine, or something else. Whatever it was, he was real touchy."

"Any blows exchanged?"

"No. Kramer told Ruther he could go straight to hell. Ruther just left the table."

"Who'd the other men side with?"

"Funny thing there. I told you Kettering and Kramer had hit it off pretty well, mainly because Kramer knew a little bit about hunting. Well, this was the day before Kettering was supposed to leave. He got pretty p.o.'d at Kramer. Told him he should have had the decency to shut up when he saw the talk was making another man sick. Kramer told *him* to go to hell, too."

"Sounds like a lovely fellow, Kramer does."

"Well, I think he knew he was on the wrong end of the argument. Lots of fellows, when they know they're wrong, they just plunge ahead and try to make it right by making it wronger."

"What happened when he told Kettering to go to hell?"

"Kettering got up from the table and said, 'Would you care to repeat that outside, Sy?' The other fellows—Miller and the old man—finally cooled off Kettering."

"Was Kramer ready to fight?"

"Sure. He was committed. The only way he could stop making an ass of himself was to make a bigger ass of himself. But I think he was glad Miller and the old man stepped in."

"What's the old man's name?"

"Murphy. John Murphy."

"He from the city, too?"

"Sure." Fielding paused. "A suburb, but that's the city, ain't it?"

"This thing between Kramer and Kettering? Did Kettering seem very angry?"

"Very. It lasted through the next day. He didn't even say good-by to Kramer when he went off into the woods."

"He did say good-by to the other men, though?"

"Yes."

"Then what happened?"

"He loaded his bags into the trunk of his car, and took off. Drove his car around the lake a ways. Said he'd head for the highway as soon as he'd bagged a few that morning. He'd come down for breakfast very early. The other men went off hunting about an hour later."

"Kramer go with them?"

"No. He went into the woods, but alone. He was pretty surly that morning. He resented Kettering's interference, and I guess he felt the other men had sided with Ruther, too. In any case, Miller and Murphy went with Ruther. Kramer went alone."

"Can we get back to Kettering for a moment?"

"Sure. I've got all the time in the world. Sure you won't stay for dinner?"

"I'm sorry, I can't. Did Kettering threaten Kramer in any way?"

"You mean . . . threaten his life?"

"Yes."

"No, he didn't. Why?"

"Do you think . . . do you think his anger was large enough to last from September to now?"

"I don't know. He was pretty damn sore at Kramer. He'd have beat him up sure if Kramer had stepped outside with him."

"Was he angry enough to *kill* Kramer?"

Fielding reflected upon this for a moment. "Kettering," he said slowly, "was a good hunter because he liked to kill. I don't hold with that kind of thinking, but that didn't make him any less a good hunter." Fielding paused. "Has Sy Kramer been killed?"

"Yes," Hawes said.

"When?"

"June twenty-sixth."

"And you think possibly Kettering waited all this time to get even for an argument that happened in September?"

"I don't know. You said Kettering was a hunter. Hunters are patient people, aren't they?"

"Kettering was patient, yes. How was Kramer killed?"

"He was shot from an automobile."

"Mmmm. Kettering was a damn good shot. I don't know."

"I don't, either." Hawes rose. "Thank you for the drink, Mr. Fielding. And thank you for the talk. You've been very helpful."

"It's been a pleasure," Fielding said. "Where are you off to now?"

"Back to the city," Hawes said.

"And then?"

"And then we'll talk to the four men who were here with

Kramer. It'd save us a little time if you had their address-es."

"I've got registry cards on all of them," Fielding said. "It doesn't take a cop to know which one you'll look up first."

"No?" Hawes said, grinning.

"No, sir. If I were Phil Kettering, I'd start getting a damn good alibi ready."

Chapter 11

Sand's Spit was a suburb of the city.

There was a time when the long finger of land served only two interests: that of the potato farmers and that of the East Shore estate owners. The farms covered most of the peninsula, rushing east and west almost to the water's edge. The estates crowded the choice waterfront sites. The farmers sowed their crops and the estate owners sowed their oats. The farmers were interested in reaping, and the estate owners were interested in sleeping. Day and night, the estates reverberated with the sound of revelry. The current Stem musical star, the tight-lipped star of silent films, producers, directors, artists, tennis players, all were entertained daily on the estates. The stars enjoyed the good clean fun on the estates. The farmers toiled in the potato fields.

And sometimes, after the sun had dropped its molten fire into the black waters of the ocean, when the potato fields rested black and silent under a pale moon, the farmers would walk down to the beach with blankets. And there they would lie on the sand and look up at the stars.

And sometimes, after the sun had dropped behind the Australian pines lining the farthermost hundred acres of an estate, after the guests had drunk their cognac and smoked their cigars, the estate owners would walk down to the beach with their guests. And there they would lie on the stars and look down at the sand.

All this was long, long ago. When the war came and it was no longer an easy thing to get help to run the twenty-five-room houses, when it was no longer an easy thing to get fuel to heat the twenty-five-room houses and the indoor tennis courts, the owners began to sell the estates—and began to discover there were no buyers for them. And shortly after the war, the potato farmers discovered they were not sitting on potato land; they were sitting on gold. An industrious builder named Isadore Morris bought the first two hundred acres of potato land for a song and built a low-cost housing development for returning veterans, naming the development "Morristown." Isadore Morris started a boom and a way of life. Other builders leaped onto the Morris bandwagon. Land that originally was priced high at two hundred dollars an acre was now going for ten thousand dollars an acre. The builders subdivided the acreage into sixty-by-a-hundred plots, and the exodus from the city to Sand's Spit was on.

Today, Sand's Spit was divided and subdivided and then divided again into small plots with small houses. The congregate Sand's Spit was a middle-income slum area with clean streets and no juvenile delinquency.

Phil Kettering lived in a Sand's Spit development known as Shorecrest Hills. There was no shore near Shorecrest Hills, nor was there the crest of a hill or even the suggestion of a hill. The development sat in almost the exact center of the peninsula on land that had once been as flat as a flapper's bosom. It was still flat. It was treeless except for the spindly silver maples the builder had magnanimously planted in the exact center of each front lawn. Shorecrest Hills. It was like calling a grimy soot-covered tenement in the 87th "Ashgrey Towers." Of such titles are million-dollar movies made.

The Kettering house was a ranch. Lest a Texan become confused, there was nothing even suggestive of a ranch about a Sand's Spit ranch. Some architect, or perhaps some builder, or perhaps some real estate agent had decided to give the title "ranch" to any house that had all of its living space on one floor. The Sand's Spit ranches did not have cattle or sheep or horses. They had, usually, three bedrooms, a living room, a kitchen, a dining room, and a bathroom. Phil Kettering lived alone in one of these Sand's Spit ranches in the development called Shorecrest Hills.

Phil Kettering, in an attempt to defy the sameness that pervaded each house in the development, had done something radical with the front yard of his house. Instead of the conventional manicured lawn, he had arranged the ground leading to the entrance doorway in a series of white gravel squares and alternating ground cover. The idea was entirely practical. Lawn mowers were going heatedly up and down the block when Carella and Hawes pulled up in the police sedan. But there was no lawn mower clicking away in Kettering's front yard—and there never would be need for a lawn mower. You can't mow gravel, and Pachysandra doesn't need trimming. Kettering had successfully reduced his yard maintenance to zero. The only thing he had to do to it was enjoy it.

On Thursday morning, July eleventh, Phil Kettering was not around to enjoy his front yard. The house was locked tighter than a miser's fist, the drapes drawn, the windows shut.

"He's probably at work," Carella said.

"Mmm," Hawes replied.

They rang the front doorbell again. Across the street, a woman looked up from her lawn mower, studying the strangers with open interest.

"Let's try the back door," Hawes said.

Together, they went around to the back of the house. The yard there was arranged in the same gravel-and-ground-cover squares. The yard was clean and still. The back door had a buzzer instead of a bell. They could hear it humming inside the house when they pressed the button. No one answered the door.

"We'd better check his office," Carella said.

"We don't know where he works," Hawes reminded him.

They came around to the front of the house again. The woman from across the street was now standing near the sedan, looking into the window. The radio was on, and the voices that erupted from it were unmistakably giving police calls. The woman listened intently, her hair in pincurls, and then backed away from the open window as the detectives approached.

"You cops?" she asked.

"Yes," Hawes said.

"You looking for Phil?"

"Yes," Hawes said.

"He ain't home."

"We know that."

"He ain't been home for quite a while."

"How long?"

"Months," the woman said. "We think he moved. Around here, we think he put the house up for sale and moved. He's the only single fellow living in the development, anyway. It's crazy for a single fellow to live here alone. Everybody else is married. The women pay too much attention to a single fellow, and the men don't like it. It's good he moved away."

"How do you know he moved away?"

"Well, he hasn't been here. So we figure he moved."

"When was he here last?"

"The fall," the woman said.

"When in the fall?"

"I don't remember. He was always coming and going. Hunting trips. He's a big hunter, Phil. He's got heads all over his living-room walls. Animal heads, I mean." She nodded. "He's a sportsman all around. Hunting, tennis. He's a good tennis player. He's got balls all over his bedroom." She looked at the detectives somewhat apologetically. "Tennis balls, I mean," she added.

"You haven't seen him since last fall?" Carella asked.

"Nope."

He looked at Hawes.

"Has his car been here?"

"Nope."

"The house has just been closed up like that?"

"Yes."

"Has anyone been around to see it?"

"What do you mean?"

"Well, you said you thought it was up for sale."

"Oh. No. No one's been to see it."

"Was there a for-sale sign up?"

"No."

"Then what makes you think it's for sale?"

"Well, Phil hasn't been here. What else would you think?"

"Is it possible Mr. Kettering has another place to live? An apartment in the city?"

"He never mentioned it."

"Was he ever away for extended periods of time before? Except on his hunting trips, I mean."

"No," the woman said.

"What bank carries his mortgage?"

"He's got no mortgage "

"How do you know?"

"Because he told us. There's only two people in the whole development who bought the house outright. Phil, and an old couple down the street. The rest of us put a down payment, and we make monthly payments to the bank. Not Phil. He put down the whole eighty-five hundred in one lump. Right after he got out of the Army. He came back from Germany with a lot of money." She looked at the detectives as if she were about to say more.

"The statute of limitations covers him," Carella said. "Besides, we're civil authorities and can't handle a military beef. Was he selling Government property on the black market?"

The woman nodded. "Sugar and coffee. He was an Army mess cook. A sergeant, I think. He used to order more than he needed and then sell it to the German people. He made a lot of money. Enough to buy this house cash, anyway."

"You're sure about that? That he has no mortgage on the house?"

"Positive."

"Which bank handles your mortgage?"

"Greater Sand's Spit Savings. There's only two banks that gave mortgages in the development. Greater Sand's Spit, and one in Isola. Banker's Trust, I think."

"We'll check those," Carella said. "Want to see what's in the mailbox, Cotton? Look into his milk box, too, will you?"

"Sure," Hawes said, and he walked toward the mailbox.

"What did you say his name was?" the woman asked.

"Whose?"

"That red-headed fellow. Your partner."

"Cotton."

"Oh," the woman said.

"Would you know if Kettering has any relations in the city? In the area?"

"He's from California originally," the woman said. "He settled here after the war, when he got back from Germany. His parents are dead, and his sister lives in Los Angeles. I don't think he gets along too well with her."

"Do they correspond?"

"I don't know. He never talks much about her."

"What's her name?"

"Susie something. He mentioned her only once. He said she was a . . . well . . ." The woman paused. "A witch. Only worse. Do you know what I mean?"

"Yes," Carella said. "Does Kettering have any lady friends?"

"He brought girls out every now and then, yes. Nice girls. Everybody in the development kept *hocking* him to get married. You know how it is." The woman shrugged. "Misery loves company."

Carella grinned. "Where does Kettering work?"

"In the city."

"Where?"

"Isola."

"What does he do?"

"He has his own business," the woman said.

"What kind of business?"

"He's a photographer."

Carella was silent for a moment. "Commercial? Portrait? What?"

"Magazine work, I think."

"How'd he drift into photography from cooking?"

"I don't know. Besides, he cooked for the Army. That isn't *real* cooking. I mean, my husband was in the Army. Did you ever eat Army food?"

"Yes," Carella said.

"So there you are. I think Phil went to school for photography after he got out of the service."

"Does he have a big business?"

"Not so. But he makes a living at it."

"Would you know where his office is?"

"Someplace in Isola. It's in the phone book. Phil Kettering."

Hawes came back from the mailbox. "Nothing in it, Steve," he said.

"Any milk?"

"Nope."

"His milk delivery stopped a long time ago," the woman said. "In fact, it was me who called the company and told them it was piling up on his back porch."

"When was this?"

"In the fall. Around October."

"Do you remember Kettering going on a hunting trip at the beginning of September?" Hawes asked.

"Is your name really Cotton?" the woman said.

"Yes."

"Oh."

"Do you remember the hunting trip?"

"Yes. He was going up to the Adirondacks someplace."

"When did he get back?"

"Well, he didn't. That was when he moved, I figure."

"He didn't come back to this house after the trip?"

"If he did," the woman said, "I didn't see him."

"Did a moving truck come around?"

"No. All his furniture's still in there."

"Who picks up his mail?"

"I don't know."

"There isn't any in the box."

"Maybe he left a forwarding address," the woman said. She shrugged.

"Do you know the names of any of his girlfriends?"

"Alice was one. I don't remember her last name. She was a nice girl. He should have married her. Then he wouldn't all the time be moving around." The woman glanced across the street. "I have to get back to my mowing. Did Phil do something?"

"You've been very helpful, Mrs.—"

"Jennings," she said. "Did Phil do something?"

"Can you direct us to the local post office?" Carella asked.

"Sure. Just drive straight into town. You can't miss it. It's right on the main street as you come into town. Did Phil do something?"

"Thank you for your time, Mrs. Jennings," Carella said. Both men got into the car. Mrs. Jennings watched them as they drove away. Then she went to her next-door neighbor and told her some cops were around asking about Phil Kettering.

"He must have done something," she told her neighbor.

The post office clerk was a harassed man trying to keep pace with the mushrooming developments on Sand's Spit.

"No sooner do we get mail service going to one development, than another one springs up," he said. "Where are we supposed to get all the mailmen? This isn't like the city, you know. In the city, a mailman steps into one apartment building and he gets rid of half his bag. Just pulls down the boxes, *zing, zing, zing,* files in the letters. Here, the mailman has to walk up the block, and he's got to go up each front walk and put the letters in the box, and then walk down the path, and then to the next house, and then *up* the path—and he picks up letters *from* the boxes, too, takes them back to the office for mailing. Half the time he's battling dogs and cats and what-not. A dame in one of the developments has a pet owl, would you believe it? The damn thing flies at the mailman's head every time he goes up that front path. It's murder. And every day there's a new damn development. We can't keep up with it."

"Do you deliver mail to a man named Phil Kettering?" Hawes asked.

"Yes!" The clerk's face lighted up. "Did you come for his mail? Did he send you for his mail?"

"We—"

"Jesus, am I glad to see you," the clerk said. "We've got mail for him stacked to the goddamn ceiling. We had to stop putting it in his box because it was falling all over the front stoop. We finally brought it all back to the office. We're hoping the stupid bastard'll contact us with a forwarding address. You should see that pile. We're not crowded enough, we've got to keep stacking his damn mail for him. Did you come for it?"

"No. But we'd like to see it."

"I can't let you take it out of this office," the clerk said. "It's addressed to him. We can't deliver it to nobody but him."

"We're cops," Carella said, and he showed his identification.

"It don't make any difference," the clerk said. "This mail is Government property. You'll need a court order to take it with you."

"Can we look at it first?"

"Sure. You've got an afternoon's work cut out for you. That stuff's been piling up since last September."

"Where is it?"

"Back there in Kettering's Korner. That's what we call it. We're thinking of starting a substation just to take care of that damn pile of mail. Why don't people leave forwarding addresses? It's the simplest thing in the world, you know. All you do is fill out a card."

"Maybe Kettering didn't want anyone to know where he was going," Hawes said.

"What reason could he have for that?"

Hawes shrugged. "Can we see the mail?"

"Sure. Come on back with me." The clerk shook his head. "It's murder. Absolute murder."

"Which is one good reason for not leaving a forwarding address," Hawes said.

"Huh?" the clerk asked.

Together, Carella and Hawes went through the stack of mail. There were circulars, bills, magazines, personal letters. The earliest postmark was August twenty-ninth. Some of the personal letters were from a man named Arthur Banks in Los Angeles. Some of the personal letters were from a woman named Alice Lossing in Isola. They copied her address from the envelope flaps. At this stage of the game, it did not seem necessary to obtain a court order granting possession of the mail.

At this stage of the game, it seemed necessary to visit Kettering's office in Isola. They thanked the clerk and went out to the automobile.

"What do you make of it?"

"You don't think he could have planned a murder as far back as September, do you?" Carella asked.

"I don't know. But why else would he disappear?"

"Maybe he hasn't. Maybe he's just changed his residence. I doubt if a guy's going to pick up and leave his business just because he had a little argument over a dinner table. Does that sound likely to you, Cotton?"

"It depends on what kind of a guy Kettering is. A patient hunter might do it. Wipe out all trace of himself, and then plan to kill Kramer. Who knows, Steve? There've been weirder ones, that's for sure."

"He's a photographer, you know. That's interesting, isn't it?"

"Yes. You thinking of the Mencken woman?"

"Um-huh."

"A guy named Jason Poole took her pictures."

"Sure. But she thinks they're in somebody else's hands now, somebody who took over from Kramer."

"Kettering?"

"Who knows? I'll tell you one thing."

"What's that?"

"I'm very anxious to talk to this guy. I think he may have a lot of the answers."

Hawes nodded. "There's just one thing, though, Steve," he said.

"Um? What's that?"

"We've got to find him first."

Chapter 12

Phil Kettering's office was on one of the side streets of midtown Isola, off Jefferson Avenue. There were a good many big and prosperous firms with offices in the building. Phil Kettering's was not one of them.

His office was at the end of the hall on the third floor, and his name was on the center of the frosted-glass door, and the word PHOTOGRAPHER was lettered in the lower right-hand corner just above the wooden portion of the door.

The office was locked.

Carella and Hawes found the superintendent of the building and asked him to open the door for them. The super had to check with the building management. It took forty-five minutes from the time of the request to the actual opening of the door.

The office was divided into three sections. There was a small room with a desk and filing cabinets in it. There was another room in which Kettering undoubtedly took his pictures. And there was a darkroom. The office did not carry the sweet smell of success. Neither did it carry any dust. Each night, the building's cleaning woman came in to empty the waste baskets and wipe off the furniture. The office was spotlessly clean. If Kettering had been there recently, the cleaning woman had wiped away all traces of his visit.

There was no mail outside the entrance doorway. There was a pile of mail inside the door, just below the mail slot. Several printed postal forms in the pile informed Kettering that the post office was holding packages too large to put through the slot. In the silence of Kettering's office, Carella and Hawes illegally opened his mail. There was nothing significant in the pile. All the letters had to do with his business. Even the manila envelopes contained photographs that were coming back from magazines. The photos were not of the cheesecake variety. Nor did any of Kettering's mail indicate that he was fond of photographing girls. His forte, apparently, was do-it-yourself pictures. Most of the correspondence was from service magazines, and all of the photos in the manila envelopes dealt with subjects like "How to Put up a Hammock," and "Refinish That Old Table!" The photos showed how to do it, step by captioned step. If there was a connection between Kettering and Lucy Mencken, it seemed rather remote at the moment.

There were some opened letters on the desk in the smallest room. The letters were dated the latter part of August. None of them had been answered. Evidently Kettering had opened these before he left for his hunting trip. Some of the new letters were letters wanting to know why a request made in August had not yet been answered.

A workbench had been set up under the lights in the studio room. A paint brush with a hole drilled through the center, a long stiff wire, and an empty coffee tin were on the center of the workbench. A plate was in the camera, loaded with film, ready to go. In the darkroom, there were negatives and prints of the first stages of the do-it-yourself project Kettering had been shooting. This one was teaching the reader how to keep a paint brush in good order by drilling a hole, putting the stiff wire through it, and using the wire to support the brush over the coffee tin without bending the bristles. The photographic essay had not been finished. Apparently Kettering's hunting trip had intruded upon its completion.

Apparently, too, Kettering had not been back to his office since last August.

Carella left the office with Hawes, and both men went down to see the building manager. The building manager was a well-groomed man in his thirties. He seemed unhurried and unruffled. His name was Colton.

"I'm going to dispossess him," Colton said. "Hell, he hasn't paid his rent for all these months. That office is losing revenue for me. I'm going to dispossess him, that's all."

"You sound as if you don't want to," Carella said.

"Well, Phil Kettering's a nice fellow. I hate like hell to throw him out into the street. But what can I do? Can I continue to lose revenue? He's skipped town, so I lose money. Is that fair?"

"How do you know he's skipped town?"

"He's not around, is he? I'm going to dispossess him, that's all. I called the building's lawyer already. We're going to post a copy of the summons and complaint on the office

door. We can stick it there with Scotch tape or with a tack,
the lawyer said. That's called 'substitute service' in this
state."

"Will you sue him for the back rent?" Hawes asked.

"How can I get a judgment for the back rent?" Colton
asked. "He has to be served papers in person for that, and
who the hell knows where he is? But I can get a judgment
evicting him. Substitute service. That's what they call it in
this state. I hate to do it to Phil, but can I lose revenue?
You can bet your life the building doesn't like to lose revenue."

"Did Kettering give you any idea he was leaving?"
Hawes asked.

"None whatever. How do you like that? Skips town.
Doesn't even have the decency to tell me he doesn't want
the office any more. What's he hiding from? Is it the police?
Is he hiding from you? Is he planning a bank robbery or
something? A murder? What? Why does the man suddenly
skip town like that? That's what I'd like to know."

Carella and Hawes nodded almost simultaneously.

Carella said it for both of them. "That's what we'd like
to know, too," he said. Then they thanked him and left his
office.

There was nothing to do but question the other men who
had been on the hunting trip.

They divided the men between them, and then Carella
and Hawes split up.

The advertising agency was called the Ruther-Smith
Company. It was a going concern, with twenty employees.
Frank Ruther was a partner in the firm, and the man who
wrote most of the company's copy.

"I'd rather be writing books," he told Hawes. "The trouble is, I can't."

He was a man in his early forties, with dark hair and
brown eyes. He did not dress at all like a Jefferson Avenue
advertising man. He dressed, instead, like the stereotyped
idea of an author, tweed jacket, soft-collared shirt, quiet tie,
dark flannel trousers. Too, like someone's stereotyped idea
of a writer—perhaps his own—he smoked a pipe. He had
greeted Hawes cordially and warmly, and they sat now in
his tastefully furnished office, talking and smoking.

"My grandfather made a hell of a lot of money," Ruther
said. "He sold pots. He traveled from town to town selling

his pots, and pretty soon he could afford to hire people to sell his pots for him. He left a lot of money to my dad."

"What did your father do" Hawes asked.

"He parlayed it into even more money. He was a dog fancier. He began importing French poodles. It doesn't sound as if there could be much money in it, but he had the biggest kennel on Sand's Spit. Quality dogs, Mr. Hawes. And my dad was a shrewd businessman. When he died, I inherited money earned by two generations of Ruthers."

"What did you do with it?"

"I wanted to be a writer. I wrote dozens of novels, which I threw into the wastepaper basket. At the same time, I was living big. I'd always lived big when my father was alive, and I saw no reason to stop living big when he died. I went through quite a lot of money. In a little less than twenty years, I spent almost the entire fortune two generations had worked to build. I stopped writing novels when I had about fifteen thousand dollars left. I started this company with Jeff Smith. It's earning its keep now. I'm beginning to feel as if I'm finally accomplishing something. It's a bad feeling, Mr. Hawes, when you know you're not accomplishing anything."

"I suppose so," Hawes said.

"A good copywriter could outline the history of my family in three words, if he wanted to. At least, the history of my family until I started this agency—when I was still fooling around writing books."

"And what are those three words?" Hawes asked.

"My grandfather, my father, and me," Ruther said. "Three generations and three occupations. The three words? A peddler, a poodler, and a piddler. I was the piddler."

Hawes smiled. He had the feeling that Ruther had used these words many times before, and that his seeming originality was not at all spontaneous. He felt, nonetheless, that it was clever—and so he smiled.

"I'm not a piddler any more, Mr. Hawes," Ruther said. "I write copy for my firm now. I write damned good copy. It sells the product. Jeff and I are making money at last. Not money I inherited. Money I worked for. Money I worked damned hard for. It's a good feeling. It's the difference between being a piddler—and a *man*."

"I see," Hawes said.

"I'm sorry," Ruther said graciously. "I didn't mean to take up your time with a family portrait."

"It was very interesting," Hawes said.

"But what did you want to know?"

"What do you know about Phil Kettering?"

"Kettering?" Ruther's brow creased. He looked at Hawes in puzzlement. "I'm sorry. I don't think I know the name."

"Phil Kettering," Hawes repeated.

"Should I know him?"

"Yes."

Ruther smiled. "Can you give me a clue?"

"Kukabonga Lodge," Hawes said.

"Oh! Oh, for God's sake, yes. Of course. Forgive me, please. I'm not good on names. Especially at that time . . . well, I was in something of a fog. I'm afraid nothing made a very clear impression on me."

"What kind of a fog?"

"My wife and I were having trouble."

"What kind of trouble?"

"Personal trouble. We thought we might split up."

"Have you?"

"No. We've worked it out. Everything is fine now."

"About Kettering. When did he leave Kukabonga?"

"Early one morning, I forget which day it was. He said he wanted to do a little shooting before hitting the road. He had his breakfast, and then left."

"Anybody go with him?"

"No, he went alone."

"Then what?"

"Well, we had our breakfast, and then we went out."

"Who?"

"Me and the two other fellows who were there. I don't remember their names."

"There were *three* other fellows, weren't there?"

"Kramer, you mean? Yes, he was the third fellow. But he didn't come with us that morning."

"Why not?"

"I'd had an argument with him the day before."

"What about?"

"Clams."

"You remember Kramer's name, don't you?"

"Yes. Because we had the argument."

"Did you see anything about him in the papers recently?"

"No. Why?"

"He's dead."

Ruther was silent for a moment. "I'm sorry to hear that," he said at last.

"Are you?"

"Yes. We'd had an argument, true, but that was a long time ago, and I was touchier than I should have been. Because of the trouble Liz and I were having. I certainly wouldn't wish his death." Ruther paused. "How did he die?"

"He was shot."

"You mean accidentally?"

"Purposely."

"Oh." Ruther paused again. "You mean he was murdered?"

"That's what I mean."

"Who did it?"

"We don't know. Have you seen Kettering since last year?"

"No. Why should I? He was a stranger. I only met him at the lodge."

"Then you wouldn't know where he is now?"

"No, of course not. Did he have something to do with Kramer's death?"

"We understand Kettering took your part in the argument and that he and Kramer almost came to blows. Is that right?"

"Yes, that's right. But that was a long time ago. You can't believe he'd harbor a grudge all this time."

"I don't know what to believe, Mr. Ruther. Can you remember the names of the other two men who were on the trip?"

"No, I'm sorry, I can't. One of them had a very strange name, but I don't remember what it was."

"I see. When did you leave the lodge?"

"On a Saturday, I think."

"Do you remember the date?"

"The eighth or the ninth, I guess. This was the first week in September."

"When did Kramer leave?"

"The same day, I think."

"And the other men?"

"We all left at the same time, I believe. We'd only gone up there for a week. I'm a little hazy on all this because I was more concerned with my wife than with hunting. The only thing I shot all the while I was there was a crow."

"Did Kettering threaten Kramer's life?"

"No. He asked him to step outside with him. That was all."

"Did he seem very angry?"

"Yes."

"Angry enough to kill?"

"I don't know."

"Mmmm."

"Why do you think Kettering killed Kramer?"

"We're not sure he did, Mr. Ruther. But he did have a possible motive, and he seems to have vanished. There's also one other thing."

"What's that?"

"Kettering was a good hunter, we've been told. Kramer was shot with a hunting rifle."

"There must be hundreds of men in this city with hunting rifles," Ruther said. "I have one myself."

"Do you, Mr. Ruther?" Hawes asked.

Ruther smiled. "Or shouldn't I have said that?"

"What kind of a gun do you own, Mr. Ruther?"

"A Marlin. Twenty-two caliber. Eight-shot."

Hawes nodded. "Kramer was killed with a .300 Savage."

"Would you like to see my gun?" Ruther asked.

"That won't be necessary," Hawes said.

"How do you know I'm not lying? I could own *two* guns, you know."

"I know. But if you killed Sy Kramer, you've probably disassembled the Savage and buried it by now."

"I suppose so," Ruther said reflectively. "I hadn't thought of that."

Hawes rose. "If you should happen to remember the names of the other two men, give me a call, won't you? Here's my card." He took the card from his wallet and put it on Ruther's desk.

Ruther looked at the card for a moment, and then said, "You knew about the argument between Kramer and me. You knew we were at Kukabonga Lodge. You knew Kettering's name, and you knew my name." He smiled. "You've been to Kukabonga Lodge, haven't you?"

"Yes."

"And you spoke with the owner, didn't you?"

"Yes."

"Then you already know the names of the other two men, don't you?"

"Yes, Mr. Ruther," Hawes said. "I already know their names."

"Then why did you ask me?"

Hawes shrugged. "Routine," he said.

"Do you think I had anything to do with Kramer's death?"

"Did you?"

"No," Ruther said.

Hawes smiled. "Then you have nothing to worry about, Mr. Ruther." He started for the door.

"Just a second, Hawes," Ruther said. There was something new in his voice, the unmistakable ring of command. The tone surprised Hawes. He turned sharply. Ruther had stood up and was coming around the desk.

"What is it, Mr. Ruther?"

"I don't like being made a fool," Ruther said. The dark eyes were darker now. The mouth was drawn into a thin line.

"Did someone make a fool of you?"

"You knew about those other two men. Were you trying to trap me?" Ruther asked.

"Trap you into what?"

For some reason the air in the office had become strained and tense. For a moment Hawes was confused, almost bewildered. The interview had gone well, smoothly. And yet, it was all changed now, and he looked at Ruther and saw a tightness about the man's face. And looking into his eyes, he felt for the moment as if Ruther would spring at his throat.

"Trap me into saying something that didn't jibe with your half-assed theories," Ruther said.

"I have no theories," Hawes said. Unconsciously he balled his fists. He expected Ruther to swing at him, and he wanted to be ready.

"Then why'd you try to trap me?"

"I didn't," Hawes said. "Mr. Ruther, you ought to know something every businessman in the world knows."

"What's that?" Ruther asked.

"How to stop when you're winning."

Ruther's face went blank. For a moment he seemed undecided. And then he smiled.

"Forgive me," he said. "It's just . . . I thought you were trying to make a fool of me."

"Let's just forget it, shall we?" Hawes said.

"Fine," Ruther said, extending his hand. "Let's just both forget it."

Hawes took the extended hand. "Sure," he said. "Let's just both forget it."

Chapter 13

John Murphy looked like a Bengal Lancer.

He had a bald pate and a white mustache and a florid complexion and a pot belly. He looked like a retired colonel who had just come back from somewhere in the British Empire. He was not a retired colonel. He was a retired broker, and he spent his time clipping coupons within the walls of an old house in New Posquit, a suburb of the city. New Posquit was not Sand's Spit. It was, as a matter of fact, in the opposite direction from Sand's Spit. The houses in New Posquit were not new, nor did they cramp each other, elbows to buttocks.

Murphy's old house rested on sixteen acres of rolling, wooded land. He was not a millionaire, but he would sooner move into an igloo than a Sand's Spit development. New Posquit had golfing clubs and tennis clubs and yacht clubs. John Murphy belonged to all of them. Perhaps he belonged to them because he was a retired man who didn't have a damned thing to do. Perhaps he belonged to them because he was a highly nervous man who couldn't even hold a gin and tonic in his hands without causing the glass to tremble.

Or maybe he was nervous because he was being questioned by a cop.

Sitting opposite him that afternoon, Steve Carella noticed the tremble in the old man's hands and wondered whether the old man could possibly hit the side of a barn on a hunting trip. Carella sat with his pad open in his lap, and he tried to take his notes effortlessly, calling as little attention to them as possible. With many people, the taking of notes became a hindrance to easy conversation. He had seen many people freeze up entirely as they watched the moving pencil. John Murphy was a highly nervous man, but Carella didn't know whether he was habitually nervous or whether the presence of a cop had brought on the trembling.

"You just live here with your family, is that it?" Carella asked.

"Yes," Murphy said. "That's what I do. Yes."

"How long have you been retired, Mr. Murphy?"

"Eleven years last month," Murphy said. "Quit when I was fifty. I'm sixty-one now."

"What do you do with your time?"

"Oh, I have things to do."

"Like what?"

"I golf. I fish. I hunt." Murphy shrugged. "I own a sports car. Raced it last year. I'm an excellent driver."

"What kind of a car?"

"A Porsche."

"Did you win the race?"

"I was in two races. Came in fourth in one, and second in the next."

"Then you *are* a good driver."

"Said so, didn't I?" Murphy said. "You want a refill on that drink?"

"No, thank you. Are you a good hunter?"

"Lousy," Murphy said. "My hands aren't too steady. I've got ulcers. That's how nervous I am." He held out his hand. "Look at that," he said.

"Mmm," Carella said. "Mr. Murphy, can you tell me about a hunting trip you took last fall? A trip to Kukabonga Lodge?"

"Certainly," Murphy said.

He began telling the story. Carella asked questions and took notes all the while. Murphy related the story of the argument over the clams, and the subsequent argument between Kramer and Kettering. His memory was excellent. He remembered all the men's names, remembered details of clothing, even mimicked some of their voices. He told the story essentially the same way Jerry Fielding had told it to Hawes up at Kukabonga. When Carella later compared his notes with Hawes, he would learn that Frank Ruther had given the same story, too.

"Ever see Kettering since that morning?" Carella asked.

"Nope."

"Been hunting since?"

"Nope."

"What kind of guns do you have, Mr. Murphy?"

"I've got three guns. A shotgun, a twenty-two, and a big-game rifle."

"What make is the big-game gun?"

"A Savage."

"Caliber?"

"Three hundred."

"May I see the gun?"

"Why?"

"I'd like to," Carella said. "I'd also like to take it with me."

"What for?"

"To hand over to our ballistics department."

"Why?"

"Sy Kramer was shot with a .300 Savage."

"I read about that in the papers," Murphy said. "Is that why you're here?"

"Yes."

"You think I shot Kramer?"

"I didn't say that, Mr. Murphy."

"I couldn't hit a grizzly bear at ten paces. You think I could have shot Kramer from a car on a dark, rainy night?"

"I didn't say that, Mr. Murphy. But I would like to have the gun run through Ballistics, if you don't mind."

"Can't you just sniff the barrel and tell it wasn't fired recently?"

Carella smiled. "We like to get a little more precise than that, Mr. Murphy. We'd like to run a comparison test between a bullet fired from your gun and the bullet that killed Kramer."

"Well, all right," Murphy said reluctantly.

"I'll give you a receipt for the gun," Carella said. "It'll be returned to you in good condition."

"Good condition isn't enough," Murphy said. "It's being turned over to you in *excellent* condition."

"You'll get it back the same way," Carella said, smiling.

"Okay," Murphy said, getting out of his chair. "It's inside, in the gun rack."

Carella followed him into the house. When Murphy had taken the Savage from the gun rack, he turned to Carella with the weapon in his hands.

"A good rifle," he said.

"Yes," Carella agreed.

"Can bring down an elephant with this," he said. Inadvertently he had turned the gun's barrel toward Carella.

"Ahhh . . . you wouldn't mind turning that the other way, would you?" Carella said.

"Why?" Murphy asked.

"I've been taught never to point a gun at anyone unless I intend shooting him."

For a moment the room went silent. Murphy stared at Carella. His finger was inside the trigger guard. His hand was trembling.

"Mr. Murphy," Carella said. "Would you mind?"

"You don't think I'd shoot you, do you, Mr. Carella?" Murphy asked. There was no smile on his face.

"No, but . . ."

"I mean, even if this *were* the rifle that killed Sy Kramer. Even *then*, do you think I'd be foolish enough to shoot you here in my own home?"

"If you're not going to shoot me," Carella said levelly, "then turn the gun away."

"Mr. Carella," Murphy said, smiling now, "I think I've made you nervous." He paused. "The gun isn't loaded." He handed it to Carella. "And it *isn't* the rifle that killed Kramer."

"I'm glad to hear both those facts," Carella said. "May I have some cartridges for the Ballistics test, please?"

"Certainly," Murphy said. He opened a drawer at the bottom of the gun rack. "I've got some full magazines here. Will they be all right?"

"Fine," Carella said.

Murphy rummaged in the drawer. "There's a pool table in the next room," he said. "Do you play pool?"

"Yes."

"Care for a game?"

"No."

"I'm glad," Murphy said. He slammed the drawer shut, and handed Carella a rotary magazine for the gun. "I'm a lousy pool player." He paused. "My hands," he explained. "They're not too steady."

And Steve Carella remembered Murphy's trembling finger inside the trigger guard.

Cotton Hawes did not realize he was being followed until he left the home of Joaquim Miller that night. When he finally realized it, he did something about it—but he was blissfully ignorant up to the moment of realization.

He had called Miller's home after leaving the office of Frank Ruther. Miller's wife told Hawes that Joaquim worked as an electronics engineer for a company called Byrd Industries, Inc. Hawes called Miller at his office. Because Miller was an employee in a large firm and because questioning by the police can often cast suspicion of guilt upon the most innocent man, Hawes considerately asked Miller if he could see him at his home that night. Miller readily agreed.

The Miller home was in Majesta, an outlying section of the city.

Hawes had left the 87th at 6:30 P.M. He pulled up to the apartment building at 8:03. He did not as yet know he had been followed from the front steps of the 87th all the way to Majesta. The apartment building in which the Millers lived was on a tree-shaded street. There was a small park across from the building. It was one of the best neighborhoods in Majesta. Hawes assumed that the Millers had chosen the location because of its proximity to the Byrd plant. And since they had chosen the best, he further assumed Miller was earning a good salary.

"Apartment Fifty-four," Miller had told him on the phone. Hawes walked across the simple lobby to the self-service elevator. He took that up to the fifth floor, and then found the Miller apartment. Mrs. Miller answered the door. She was an attractive brunette with large blue eyes, but Hawes made a point of never falling in love with a woman who was already married.

"Are you Detective Hawes?" she asked immediately.

"Yes." Hawes showed his identification.

"Is something wrong?"

"No. We're just trying to locate a man your husband once met. We thought he might be able to help."

"It's nothing to do with Joaquim?"

"No, ma'am," Hawes said.

"Come in, won't you?" she answered, and he had the distinct impression that if this had had something to do with Joaquim, she'd have slammed the door in his face and then fired a machine-gun volley through it. The protective Mrs. Miller led Hawes into the living room. Joaquim Miller turned from the television set.

"This is Detective Hawes," his wife said.

Miller rose, his hand extended. He was a thin man of about thirty-three, with a narrow face topped with a brown crew cut. His eyes were warm and intelligent. His grip on Hawes's hand was firm.

"Glad to meet you, Mr. Hawes," he said. "Have you found him yet?"

"No, not yet," Hawes replied.

"They're looking for a man named Phil Kettering," Miller explained to his wife. "Mr. Hawes told me about it on the phone this afternoon."

Mrs. Miller nodded. Her eyes did not leave Hawes's face.

"Sit down, Mr. Hawes," Miller said. "Can we get you something to drink?"

"No, thank you."

"Glass of beer? You're allowed a glass of beer, aren't you?"

"I'd rather not, thank you."

"Okay, then," Miller said. "What would you like me to tell you?"

"Everything you remember about Phil Kettering and Sy Kramer," Hawes said.

Miller began talking, and while he talked Hawes took notes and thought, "Police work is simply getting everything in triplicate." Miller was telling the same story Fielding had told, the same story Ruther had told, the same story Murphy had given to Carella earlier that day. It was getting a little boring, to tell the truth. Hawes wished for some outstanding deviation from the facts, something he could pounce on. There was no deviation. Miller told the story straight down the line.

"Have you seen Kettering since?" Hawes asked.

"Since the day he left the lodge?" Miller asked.

"Yes," Hawes said.

"No, I haven't."

"Do you own a gun, Mr. Miller?"

"No."

"You don't?"

"No, sir."

"Didn't you hunt on that—"

"I rented that gun, Mr. Hawes. I'm not a real hunter, you see. Peg was visiting her mother in California. We don't get along, Peg's mother and me. She didn't want Peg to marry me, but we got married, anyway."

"She didn't think Joaquim would amount to anything. But he's amounted to a lot."

"Please, Peg," Miller said.

"Well, you have. He earns a very good salary, Mr. Hawes. We've been able to save quite a bit between his salary and the land."

"Peg, can't you—?"

"What land?" Hawes asked. "What do you mean?"

Miller sighed. "I speculate," he explained. "I buy and sell land. With all these housing developments springing up all over the place, it's been pretty profitable."

"How do you work it?"

"Sheer speculation. I pick a spot I think the developers will eventually get to. I buy it fairly cheap, and then sell it high when they decide to build on it. It won't last much longer, though. They've pretty much built everywhere they *can* build and still stay within reasonable commuting distance of the city."

"How much have you made with such speculation?" Hawes asked.

"That's our business," Miller said.

"I'm sorry," Hawes said. "I didn't mean to get personal, but I would like to know."

"We've made about thirty thousand," Miller's wife said.

"Peg—"

"Well, why shouldn't we tell?"

"Peg, shut—"

"We're saving it," Mrs. Miller said. "We're going to build a big house some—"

"*Shut up, Peg!*" Miller snapped.

Mrs. Miller fell into a resentful silence. Hawes cleared his throat.

"What kind of work do you do with Byrd, Mr. Miller?"

"I'm an electronics engineer."

"I know. But what are you working on?"

Miller smiled as if his team had scored a point. "I couldn't answer that one if I wanted to."

"Why not?"

"Classified," Miller said.

"I see. Just to reiterate—you do not own a gun, is that correct?"

"That's absolutely correct."

"What kind of a gun did you rent when you went away?"

"A twenty-two."

"Would you remember what kind of a gun Kettering was using?"

"I'm not good on guns," Miller said. "It was a big-game rifle—a powerful name. A name that sounded like a big-game gun."

"A Savage?" Hawes asked.

"Yes," Miller said. "Kettering was using a Savage."

In the street again, Hawes glanced up at the apartment building. He saw Miller standing at the window, watching him. He ducked away from the window quickly when he realized Hawes had seen him. Hawes sighed and started for his car. It was then that he saw the man. The man moved behind a tree quickly, but not quickly enough. Hawes had caught a glimpse of him, and he walked to his car slowly now, opened the door, started the engine, and waited. The man did not move from behind the tree. Hawes set the car in motion. From the corner of his eye, he saw the man run for an automobile and enter it. The car was a Chevrolet, but Hawes could not distinguish the license-plate number in the darkness. Behind him, he heard the car starting.

He drove slowly. His pursuer did not know that Hawes knew he was being pursued. Hawes did not want the pursuer to lose him, nor did he wish to lose the pursuer. There was, of course, the added possibility that the man was not following him at all. Hawes would test this possibility in a moment.

He waited until he'd picked up the man's headlights in the rear-view mirror. Up to that point, he had been driving slowly, as if unsure of which turn to take. Now he sped up, turned left, and watched the car behind him execute the same turn. He turned right. The Chevy turned right. He went straight for two blocks, and then made a left. The Chevy was still behind him. He executed a series of lefts and rights that eliminated all possibility of chance. The man in the Chevy was certainly following Hawes, and Hawes wondered why. He also wondered who. He could not see the front license plate in his rear-view mirror. He wanted to know who the hell was in that car.

He put on a sudden burst of speed, outdistancing the Chevy by a block, and then pulled over to the curb. He got out of the car and ducked into the nearest alley. Up the street, the Chevy braked suddenly and then pulled to the curb a distance behind Hawes's car. The man got out of the car, looked up and down the street, and then began walking toward the alley.

The luxuriant summer growth on the trees shielded the street lamps so that the sidewalks were in almost total darkness. Hawes could hear the man's footsteps as he approached, but he could not see the man's face. The man had undoubtedly assumed that Hawes had gone into one of the apartment buildings. He stopped at each entrance and looked into the building, moving closer to the alleyway all the time.

The footsteps echoed in the hollow bowl of night.

Hawes waited.

They were closer now, very close, almost, almost. . .

Hawes reached out, swinging the man around.

The man moved with a reflexive action that caught Hawes completely by surprise. Hawes was no midget, and certainly bigger than the man who hit him. But he had reached out with one hand, grasping the man by the shoulder, and the man had swung around, partially pulled by Hawes, partially under his own power, so that the force of his blow was doubled.

He swung around with his fist clenched, and he threw the fist at Hawes's midsection, catching him below the belt. The pain was excruciating. Hawes released the man's shoulder instantly and dropped to the concrete. The man ran out of the alley mouth. Hawes had still not seen his face. Lying on the concrete, raw pain triggering through his groin, he could only think of a stupid joke he had once heard. He did not want to think of the joke. He wanted to get up off the concrete and chase his assailant, but the pain persisted in agonizing waves, and the joke ran over and over again in his mind, the joke about a man overhearing two women describing childbirth to each other. "Such pain," one said. "Nobody ever had such pain as when I gave birth."

"Pain? Don't talk about pain," the other woman said. "When my Lewis was born, it was unbearable. Such pain no one in the world has ever known."

And the man walked over to them and said, "Excuse me, ladies, but did either of you ever get kicked in the balls?"

There didn't seem to be anything funny about the joke now. Lying on the concrete, Hawes knew only pain, and the joke was not funny at all. Lying on the concrete, he could hear the Chevy's motor starting. He dragged himself to the alley mouth, hoping to catch a glimpse of the license plate as the car went by.

The street was dark, and the car wasn't observing any speed limits.

Hawes could not read the plate.

In a little while, the pain subsided.

Steve Carella didn't truthfully suspect John Murphy. He didn't know whom he truthfully suspected at this stage of the game, but he did know that the man who'd fired the Savage at Kramer had been a dead shot. Only one shell had been fired, and that shell had blown away half of Kramer's head. Whoever had killed Kramer had been driving an automobile not a minute before—or so it appeared. He had pulled the car to the curb, picked up the rifle, aimed, and fired. His aim had been unerring. The single shot had done it.

Carella doubted that John Murphy's aim was unerring. The old man's hands trembled even when he was sitting having a peaceful drink. If they trembled normally, how much more would they tremble when murder was about to be done? No, he did not truthfully suspect John Murphy.

He was not at all surprised, therefore, by the Ballistics report on the test bullet fired from Murphy's .300 Savage.

The Ballistics report simply stated that the gun owned by John Murphy could not possibly have fired the bullet that had killed Kramer.

Steve Carella was not at all surprised—but he was disappointed, anyway.

Chapter 14

Alice Lossing lived in Isola.

Cotton Hawes had been hit uncompromisingly the night before, but on the evening of July twelfth he nonetheless went to visit Miss Lossing. The apartment building was on The Bluffs, overlooking the River Dix. The River Dix bounded Isola on the south, and from Alice Lossing's building, Hawes supposed you could see the prison at Walker's Island on a clear day.

He stopped at Apartment 8B and buzzed.

"Who is it?" a girl's voice called from within the apartment.

Hawes hesitated. He could remember his indoctrination into the 87th Precinct. He had knocked on the door of a suspected murderer and then had said, "Police! Open up!" The man inside had opened up with a pistol, and a cop named Steve Carella had almost been killed that day. Even now, Hawes flushed slightly at his earlier stupidity. But Alice Lossing was not suspected of murder.

"Police," he said.

"Who?"

"Police," he repeated.

"Just a second," the voice said. He heard footsteps approaching the door. The flap in the door swung back. An eye appeared in the circle.

"Who'd you say you were?"

"Police," Hawes said. "Detective Hawes."

"Have you got identification?"

"Yes."

"Let me see it?"

Hawes held up his plastic-encased I.D. card.

"Haven't you got a badge?"

Hawes held up his shield.

The girl looked at the I.D. card again. "You don't look very much like the picture," she said.

"It's me. If you want further proof, call Frederick 7-

117

8024. Ask for Detective Carella, and ask him if Detective Cotton Hawes did not leave the squadroom on his way to visit you."

"It sounds convincing," Alice said. "Just a second."

Hawes listened while the girl unlatched the door. From the number of bolts being snapped back, it sounded as if he were being admitted to Fort Knox. He wondered why the girl was so damned cautious, and then the door opened and he knew why.

Alice Lossing was perhaps the most beautiful girl he'd seen all week long. If he were Alice Lossing and if he lived in an apartment building, he would surely have constructed a steel door to keep away the wolves.

"Come in," she said. "You'd better be legit."

"Why?"

"I keep a pistol, and I know how to shoot it."

"Do you keep a rifle?" he asked, from force of habit.

"No, thanks. A pistol serves the purpose just dandy."

"The best weapon for a woman is a hammer," Hawes said.

"A what?"

"A hammer."

"Come in, come in. If you're going to discuss weapons, don't stand there in the doorway."

Together, they went into the apartment. Alice Lossing had brown hair and brown eyes. She was a tall girl, at least five-seven, and she walked with the regal splendor of a queen. Her figure was neatly curved beneath the tapered slacks and sweater she wore.

When they were in the living room, she asked, "Why a hammer?"

"Several reasons. One, the excitability of a woman. Faced with an intruder, she may not shoot straight. She'll empty the pistol, and then be left holding an empty weapon, which makes a clumsy club."

"I shoot straight," Alice said.

"Two, an intruder seeing a gun may pull his own gun, if he's carrying one. Chances are, he'll shoot straighter than the woman."

"I shoot straight," Alice repeated.

"Three, if an intruder has rape on his mind, he's got to come close to do it. A hammer is a good infighting weapon. If he's just got robbery or burglary on his mind, the best thing to do is let him take what he wants and then call the police. A gun might start trouble where there wouldn't have been any trouble. Nobody gets heroic with a hammer. A hammer is purely a weapon of defense."

"Is that your case?"

"Yes," Hawes said.

"It stinks," Alice said. "I keep a pistol in my night table, and it's loaded, and I'll shoot any person who steps into this apartment without being invited. I'll shoot him straight and true and probably dead."

"A girl can't be too careful," Hawes said. "Especially a pretty girl. I'm glad I was invited."

"What's this about?" Alice asked. "I'm purposely ignoring your compliment."

"Why?"

"You're too attractive," Alice said. "I might lose my head and shoot off my big toe by accident." She grinned.

"Exactly my point," Hawes said, returning the grin.

"What *is* this about?"

"Phil Kettering," Hawes said.

"What about him? Where is he? Do you know?"

"We don't know. He seems to have vanished."

"Don't I know it," Alice said.

"When'd you see him last?"

"In August of last year."

"Haven't heard from him since?"

"No," Alice said. "I wouldn't give a damn, but he's got something that belongs to me."

"What?"

"A ring."

"How'd he get it?"

"I gave it to him. We got drunk together one night, and we decided to exchange rings. He gave me this piece of cheese"—she held out her right hand—"and I gave him a damn expensive cocktail ring. He wore it on his pinky."

"May I see that again?" Hawes said.

Alice extended her hand. The ring was a simple signet, the letters *P.K.* in gold scroll, with a small diamond chip near the *K*.

"I had it appraised," Alice said. "Fifty bucks, the jeweler told me. My ring was worth five hundred. If you find him, tell him I want that damn ring back."

"How well did you know Kettering?"

"Not very."

"Well enough to give him a ring?"

"We were drunk. I told you."

"How long did you know him?"

"About four months. I'm a receptionist at *Milady*. Do you know the magazine?"

"No," Hawes said.

"The women of America only wake up and go to sleep with the damn thing," Alice said.

"I'm sorry."

"You should be. I thought cops were well-informed. Anyway, I'm the receptionist there. Phil came up one day to deliver some pictures. A photographic essay on how to keep nail-polish bottles in one place. He had this long piece of wood with spaces drilled into it—"

"Is that when you met?"

"Yes. He asked me out. I accepted. I went out with him about once a week after that."

"Up until the time he went on his hunting trip?"

"Is that where he went? He didn't tell me."

"Did he ever discuss hunting with you?"

"Once in a while. He was pretty good, to hear him tell it."

"How good?"

"Won a lot of shooting medals. Supposed to be a crack shot. That's the way he told it, anyway."

"Did you ever see any of those medals?"

"One. He carried it in his wallet. It was a shooting medal, all right. I guess he *was* a good hunter."

"Did he call you when he got back from the trip?"

"I haven't seen or heard from him since the end of August. I wrote him several letters asking for my ring back. He never answered them. I called his office, and I even went down there. The place was locked up. If I could remember where he lives, I'd go there, believe me."

"Forget it," Hawes said. "We've been."

"Then he's really gone?"

"Really gone," Hawes said.

"Where?"

"We don't know."

"Well, I'd sure like to know. That ring was worth five hundred dollars."

"Is he a good-looking man, Miss Lossing?"

"Phil? Not in the movie-star sense. But he's very manly-looking."

"Have a temper?"

"Not particularly violent, no."

"Is he the kind of person who'd be likely to carry a grudge?"

"I don't think so. I don't know him that well. We only dated for about four months, once a week. The only reason we exchanged rings is because we were drunk."

"Did you go out to his home often?"

"I was there once. It's a real suburban nothing. I ran for the hills."

"Did he ever come here?"

"Of course."

"Often?"

"To pick me up. Once a week. And to drop me off." Alice Lossing studied Hawes for a moment. "What are you asking?"

"Only what I asked."

"Are you trying to find out whether Phil and I—"

"No."

"We didn't."

"Okay, but I didn't ask."

"You seemed like you wanted to."

"Ask?"

"Yes."

"*About* Phil? Or *for* myself?"

"One or the other," Alice said.

"I'm not an asker," Hawes said.

"No?"

"No. I have to report back to the squad when I leave here. I can do that by phone. Do you dance?"

"I dance."

"Let's."

"Are you asking?"

Hawes smiled. Alice Lossing did not smile back.

"I'm a lady," she said. "I like to be asked."

"I'm asking. Would you like to go dancing with me?"

"You're attractive," she said. "I'd love to."

"I keep wondering what a pretty girl like you is doing home all alone on a Friday night," Hawes said.

"I was waiting for you," Alice answered.

"Sure."

"If you want to know the truth, I was stood up."

"Okay."

"You can call the squad from here, if you like. I'll get changed."

"Fine."

"Are you off-duty once you make that call?"

"Technically, I'm never off-duty. But actually, yes, I am."

"Then mix yourself a drink when you're finished."

"All right."

Hawes made his call and mixed himself a drink. They left the apartment at nine-thirty. Alice thought Hawes was very attractive. She kept telling him so all night long. He thought she was very attractive, too. In fact, he fell in love with her while they were dancing.

They went for coffee afterward, and then he took Alice back to her apartment. It was still early, and so they sat and listened to records for a while. Her lips were very red and very inviting, and so he kissed her. It was too bright in the room, and so they turned off the lights.

And so . . .

Chapter 15

Arthur Brown was tired of the virgins of Bali in full color. He was tired of the four wooden walls of the mock telephone-company shack. He was tired of the headset with which he monitored the tape. He was tired of the inane social drivel that passed back and forth between Lucy Mencken and her contacts in the world at large.

Arthur Brown was a most impatient man. He'd had the bad misfortune to be born with a name that emphasized his color. With Arthur Brown, the hatemongers had really had a field day. Because he was fair-minded and because he thought it might be better to give the haters an edge by giving himself a handicap, he had often thought of changing his name to Goldstein, thereby adding religion to color and offering the haters an opportunity to really flip their wigs. His impatience was born of expectation. Arthur Brown could look at a man and know instantly whether or not his color would be a barrier between them. And knowing, he would then expect the inevitable slur; and expecting it, he would then impatiently wait for it. He was a man sitting on a powder keg, the fuse of which had been lighted by the chance pigmentation of his skin.

The tap on Lucy Mencken's phone had none of the characteristics of a powder keg, but it nonetheless filled Brown with itchy impatience. He could, by now, have told anyone interested exactly what the Mencken family would be having for dinner every night of next week, exactly what sniffles or sneezes the Mencken children had suffered during the past few days, the forthcoming social plans of the entire family, and even the bra size—a spectacular size, he admitted—of Lucy Mencken.

Arthur Brown was bored.

Arthur Brown was impatient.

He thought of his brothers of toil back at the 87th. Those lucky ones would be dealing with rapes and muggings and knifings and burglaries and robberies and homicides and all sorts of interesting lively criminal activities. He had to sit in a shack and listen to the proprietress of the women's wear shop in Peabody—he knew her well by now; her name was Antoinette, and the shop was sickeningly called the Curve Corner—tell Lucy Mencken about the new line of bathing suits that had arrived, and wouldn't she like to come down and try some on?

Brown devoutly wished she would go down and try some on. He wished she would take her son and daughter with her and allow them to try on some bathing suits, too. He hoped that Charles Mencken needed new swim trunks. He hoped the entire family would go down to the Curve Corner and enjoy an orgy of trying on svelte swimwear. Then the phone would be free for the afternoon. Then he would not have to listen to female gossip about a girl named Patricia Harper who danced too intimately with the husband of Peabody; then he would not have to listen to plans for the next garden-club meeting (the club was called the Peabody Potters); then he would not have to listen to eight-year-old Greta's telephone romance with a ten-year-old boy named Freckles.

In short, he would not have to invade the goddamn privacy of what seemed to be a normal, decent, clean-living family.

He knew, of course, that the telephone company itself maintained monitoring stations. The purpose of these stations was to keep a constant check on the efficiency of the almost entirely automatic equipment. There was no intention of maintaining a *telephone tap* in the strictest sense of the words. But there *were* loud-speakers, and men listened to those loud-speakers, and if anyone thought a telephone call was a private thing, he was sadly mistaken. Usually, the speaker was tuned down to a low mumble. Occasionally, and completely arbitrarily, it was turned up so that words became intelligible. A telephone call was about as private as a church auction, and this should have lessened the guilt Brown was feeling. Too, he was waiting for a call that might lead them to a criminal. But neither of these factors lessened the unpleasantness of his job, nor the impatience with which he attacked it.

When the call came, he girded himself for what he was certain would be another social exchange. The light flashed on the recording equipment as soon as the receiver was lifted from the cradle in the Mencken home. Brown put on his earphones. Before him, the tapes wound relentlessly. The bug in the base of the Mencken phone picked up every word.

"—wait a moment, I'll see if she's home."

That was the Mencken maid. Brown knew her voice by heart. There was a long pause. Then . . .

"Hello?"

"Mrs. Mencken?"

Brown heard what could have been a short gasp from Mrs. Mencken.

"Yes?"

"You've had time to think over my last call, ain't you?"

"Who is this?" Lucy asked.

"Never mind who this is. I told you this is a friend of Sy Kramer's. I know all about the arrangement he had with you, and I've already told you there will be a few changes now that he is dead. Is that clear?"

"Yes, but . . ."

"You wouldn't want that material released to the newspapers, would you?"

"What material?"

"Don't bluff me, Mrs. Mencken. You know what material I'm talking about, so don't try to bluff me."

"All right," she said.

"I want you to meet me tonight."

"Why? Just give me your name, and I'll send you the check."

"You'll send a policeman to pick me up, you mean."

"No, I wouldn't do that."

"You'd be smart not to try anything like that. The material is with a friend of mine. If you try to call the police, if there's even the smell of a cop with you when we meet tonight, that stuff gets mailed to the newspapers."

"I understand. But why must we meet?"

"To get things set up."

"You said it would be about the same as with Kramer."

"I want to talk it over with you. I want to know just where we stand. I don't want any mistakes."

"All right," Lucy said wearily. "Where shall I meet you?"

"Can you get in to the city?"

"Yes."

"Do you know downtown Isola?"

"Yes."

Brown picked up his pencil and moved his pad into writing position.

"There's a place on Fieldover Street. Do you know where that is?"

"In the Quarter?"

"Yes. The place is called Gumpy's. It's right on Fieldover, near Marsten Square. I'll meet you there."

"What time?"

"Eight o'clock?"

"Yes," Lucy said. "How will I know you?"

"I'll be wearing a brown sharkskin suit." The man paused. "I'll be reading the *Times*. Remember, no cops. If there are any cops, the material gets mailed out before you can say Jack Robinson."

"I'll be there," Lucy promised.

"Bring your checkbook," the man said, and he hung up.

The next call Lucy Menckin made was to her husband's office. She told Charles Mencken that a college roommate of hers, a girl named Sylvia Cooke, was in town and wanted Lucy to join her for the evening. Would it be all right?

Charles Mencken was a trusting husband with a faithful wife. He told Lucy it would be perfectly all right. In fact, he would take the children to the country club for dinner. She told him she loved him, and then broke the connection.

Arthur Brown immediately called the 87th Squad.

Gumpy's could just as easily have been called Dumpy's, because it was just that. Whoever had made the call to Lucy Mencken had shown considerable unconcern for the fact that she was a lady. The person who'd called her had even shown unconcern for the fact that she was a woman.

Gumpy's was on Fieldover Street, close to Marsten Square. Gumpy's catered to the trade in the Quarter. The trade did not care very much about the furniture in Gumpy's, or the lighting, or the fact that the walls seemed ready to cave in. The trade was neither here nor there, and the trade was more or less protected by a state law that made a token show of force while actually overloooking the neither here nor there status of such people as composed the clientele of Gumpy's. Many people from other places in the city came to ogle the steady clientele of Gumpy's. It was good clean fun to howl at two men dancing together. It was excruciatingly comic to see a woman wearing a man's suit and paying court to another woman. These sightseers, like the steady clientele, were too interested in what was happening around them to pay too much attention to the décor of the place. Even the fire inspector didn't care very much. It was rumored about that Gumpy himself paid a considerable chunk each month to keep the place from being condemned as a fire trap. Such rumors always run rife when a man has a profitable enterprise going for him. Why, the fire inspector may have been the most honest man in the city, and far above taking any sort of bribe.

The detective who went to Gumpy's in a sports shirt and slacks on the night of July thirteenth was a man who had no connection with the Kramer case at all. In debating who should make the collar, Carella and Hawes weighed in the fact that Hawes had been tailed not two nights before. It was possible, just possible, that the tail would turn out to be the person who had the assignation with Lucy Mencken. And if Hawes had been tailed, was it not likely that other members of the squad had likewise been tailed and could likewise be recognized? They did not want to lose a collar by being spotted for bulls. They chose a man who'd done no legwork on the Kramer case, a man in fact who'd just polished off a burglary and who was waiting for action.

The man's name was Bob O'Brien. He was a Detective 2nd/Grade. He was Irish clear down to his belly button. Some of the bulls held that the only reason he'd joined the force was so that he'd be able to march in the St. Paddy's Day parade down Hall Avenue. Actually, O'Brien had joined the force quite by accident. He'd applied for positions as postal clerk, fireman, and cop; he'd passed all three examinations. By pure chance, the police department had called him first, and he'd taken the job.

O'Brien was six feet one inch tall and he weighed two hundred and ten pounds. When you got hit by O'Brien, you sometimes suffered a fractured jaw. The hamhock-hands cliché had been invented to apply to the Irish mitts of Bob O'Brien. He'd been raised in Hades Hole, and had learned the art of street fighting (as opposed to the art of boxing) before he'd cut his second teeth. In those days, O'Brien had been on the opposite side of the law. When you saw a cop coming, you ran like hell. Now, and fortunately for the city, he was on the right side of the fence, using his fists for law enforcement, using his 20/20 vision and his .38 Police Special to excellent advantage.

Bob O'Brien had killed seven men in the line of duty.

He was not a trigger-happy cop. He never used his gun unless he had to. But there are cops who get the dirty end of the stick, cops who are *forced* to use their gun, and Bob O'Brien was one of those cops. He had killed his first man when he was still a rookie, and the first man he'd killed was a man he'd known. He had still been living in Hades Hole at the time. It was a Saturday morning in mid-August, and O'Brien was off-duty and wearing a pair of swimming trunks under his slacks and sports shirt. He was supposed to meet a few of the fellows on his front stoop. From there the boys would go to the beach. He was, of course, carrying a gun in his right hip pocket. The street was quiet with the hush of a hot summer. O'Brien loafed on the front stoop, waiting for the boys. It was then that Eddie the Butcher came out of his shop with the meat cleaver.

Eddie was chasing a woman. On his face was the crazed look of a man who has lost all touch with his surroundings. O'Brien came off the stoop as the woman rushed by. He stepped directly into Eddie's path. He had no intention of shooting Eddie.

"What's the matter, Eddie?" he said gently.

Eddie raised the meat cleaver over his head. "Get out of my way!" he shouted.

"This is Bobby," O'Brien said. "Now put away that—"

Eddie lunged forward, knocking O'Brien flat to the pavement. With one hand holding O'Brien's throat, he raised his other hand over his head, and the cutting edge of the meat cleaver gleamed in the morning sunlight. O'Brien twisted onto one hip. The crazed expression was still on Eddie's face. The meat cleaver was poised above O'Brien's head. And then it began its shimmering descent. O'Brien, acting reflexively, drew his revolver, and fired. The cleaver dropped from Eddie's hand, six inches from O'Brien's face. Eddie rolled over onto the scorching pavement—dead.

That night Bob O'Brien cried like a baby.

And since that time death had hung around his neck like an albatross. Since that time he had been forced to kill six more men in the line of duty. He did not know any of these men, but that was the only difference between them and Eddie the Butcher. Whenever he was forced to kill, Bob O'Brien still wept. Not openly. He wept inside, and that is where it hurts most.

Gumpy's was jumping that Saturday night. In the space of twenty minutes, O'Brien was approached and propositioned five times. He turned down each proposition. He felt only pity for Gumpy's clientele, and so he turned down each proposition with a simple shake of his head. The people he despised were those who came to watch the display.

At eight ten, Lucy Mencken arrived.

She seemed quite flustered, quite beyond her depth. She sat at a table in the corner and instantly surveyed the room. The man in the brown sharkskin suit had not yet arrived. She ordered a drink and waited. O'Brien ordered a drink, which he did not touch, and he, too, waited.

At eight twenty-five the man in the brown sharkskin suit entered the bar. A copy of the *Times* was rolled under his right arm. He looked around, his eyes passing over Lucy Mencken and then the rest of the room. Then he went to sit at her table. A few words passed between Lucy and the man.

O'Brien got off the bar stool. Casually he walked to the table. Casually he caught the man's brown sharkskin sleeve with his right forefinger, twisting the sleeve, capturing the man's wrist in a makeshift handcuff.

"Police," he said flatly. "You're coming with—"

The man started to get out of his chair. O'Brien very casually hit him. The clientele of Gumpy's started an ungodly shriek.

"Go home, Mrs. Mencken," O'Brien said. "We'll take care of him."

Lucy Mencken surveyed O'Brien with a hard, flat stare. "Thanks," she said, "you've just ruined my life."

The man in the sharkskin suit was Mario Torr.

In the Interrogation Room of the 87th Precinct, he said, "This is false arrest. I don't even know why I'm here."

"We know why you're here," Carella said.

"Yeah? Then suppose you tell me why. I'm an honest citizen. I'm gainfully employed. I stop into a place for a brew, I see a pretty dame, I try to pick her up, and next thing I know I'm getting the rubber hose."

"Has anybody laid a finger on you, Torr?" Hawes asked.

"Well, no, but—"

"Then shut your mouth and answer the questions!" Meyer snapped contradictorily.

"I *am* answering the questions. And somebody *did* lay a finger on me. That lousy big Irish bastard who put the collar—"

"You resisted arrest," Carella said.

"I resisted, my ass. I just got out of the chair. He didn't have to hit me."

"What were you doing in Gumpy's?" Meyer asked.

"I told you. I stopped in for a brew."

"Do you always go to fag joints?" Carella asked.

"I didn't know what kind of a joint it was. I passed it, so I stopped in for a brew."

"You called Lucy Mencken this afternoon, didn't you?"

"No."

"We've got a tape of the whole telephone conversation."

"It must have been three other guys," Torr said.

"Where are the pictures?"

"What pictures?"

"The pictures you were using to extort money from Lucy Mencken."

"I don't know what you're talking about."

"Did you follow me the other night?" Hawes asked.

"I didn't follow nobody any night."

"You followed me and hit me. Why?"

"*I* hit *you?* Don't be ridiculous."

"Where are the pictures?"

"I don't know anything about pictures."

"Were you and Kramer partners?"

"We were friends."

"Did you kill him to get him out of the set-up?"

"Kill him! Holy Jesus, don't tie me into that rap!"

"Which rap do you want, Torr? We've got a lot of them."

"I had nothing to do with the Kramer kill. So help me Jesus."

"We can make it look pretty good, Torr."

"You ain't got a chance."

"Haven't we? Try us. What'll you go for? Extortion or homicide?"

"I stopped for a brew," Torr insisted.

"We've got your voice on tape."

"Try to make that stick in court."

"Where are the pictures?"

"I don't know anything about pictures."

"Why'd you follow me?" Hawes asked.

"I didn't follow you."

"The tape said you'd be wearing a brown sharkskin suit.

It said you'd be reading the *Times*. Guess what you're wearing, and guess what you were carrying."

"It ain't admissible in court," Torr said.

"Who were the big marks?" Meyer hurled.

"I don't know."

"Kramer's bank account had forty-five grand in deposits. Was that only half of it, Torr? Did the total amount to ninety grand?"

"Forty-five grand?" Torr said. "So that's—"

"What?"

"Nothing."

"That's *what?*"

"Nothing."

"Was Lucy Mencken paying more than the five bills a month?"

"Is that all she—?" Torr stopped abruptly.

"Hold it," Hawes said.

The other men looked at him.

"Hold it a minute." The light of pure inspiration was on his face. "This son of a bitch doesn't even know how much Lucy Mencken was paying! I'll bet he doesn't even know for *what* she was paying. You didn't know there *were* pictures, did you, Torr?"

"I told you already. I don't know nothing about it."

"You son of a bitch," Hawes said. "You've been conducting your own little investigation, haven't you? You've been following the bulls of this squad to get onto Kramer's marks!"

"No, no, I—"

"The only thing you knew was that there *were* marks. And with Kramer dead, you figured to latch onto them. But you didn't know who or how much."

"No, no, I told you—"

"You followed us to Lucy Mencken and then called her to say you were taking over from Kramer. She was so scared she automatically assumed you knew all about the pictures. That was when she began snooping around, trying to locate them. Kramer was something she knew how to deal with. But you told her there'd be changes, and she didn't know how far you were planning to go—and so she made a last try to get those photos."

"I don't know what you're—"

"When you followed me the other night, you were looking for more of Kramer's marks."

"You're crazy."

"How does this sound, Torr? You knew Kramer had a sweet deal, and you wanted it. You were tired of being a laborer, earning whatever the hell you earned a week. You wanted the big loot. Kramer probably talked a lot about big living. You were green with envy. You got a rifle, and you got a car. And then you—"

"No!"

"You killed him," Hawes said.

"I swear—"

"You killed him," Carella shouted.

"No, for Christ's sake, I—"

"YOU KILLED HIM!" Meyer bellowed.

"No, no, I swear to God. I followed you, yes, almost every one of you, yes, I hit you the other night, yes, I tried to get in on the Mencken squeeze, yes, yes, but Jesus Christ, I didn't kill Kramer. I swear to God, I didn't kill him."

"You tried to extort money from Lucy Mencken?" Hawes asked.

"Yes, yes."

"You hit me the other night?"

"Yes, yes."

"Book him for extortion and felonious assault," Hawes said.

Torr seemed happy it was all over.

Chapter 16

It seemed evident at this point that Lucy Mencken and Edward Schlesser, the soda-pop man, had no further worries. Neither did the third, eleven-hundred-dollar mark who had contributed monthly to Kramer's checking account. Extending this further, now that Kramer was dead and the sham extortionist Torr exposed, the big mark had nothing to fear, either. The big mark who had furnished Kramer's apartment, bought his cars, and paid for his clothes, and then swelled his bank account to $45,000 was off the hook. Kramer was dead. No one had inherited his lucrative racket.

Everybody should have been extremely happy, and perhaps they all were. Everybody but the cops.

Kramer was dead, and someone had killed him, and that spelled homicide. And the cops still didn't know who or why.

Every post office in the city had been checked, as well as every bank. Unless Kramer had kept a box under an unknown alias, it seemed fairly certain the documents were being kept elsewhere. Kramer was a precise man who kept bills going back as far as last September. It did not seem likely that he would have been sloppy in the matter of keeping important papers and photographs. But where?

His apartment had been searched by a crew of four detectives who worked for two days going over every inch of the place. Nancy O'Hara's presence did not help the search. She was a mighty pretty girl, and cops are human. But the search was nonetheless a thorough one, and it turned up neither the missing documents nor a key to a possible deposit box somewhere in the city.

"I don't know," Carella said to Hawes. "The whole goddamn thing seems to have bogged down."

"He's got to have them someplace," Hawes said.

"Where? He doesn't belong to any clubs."

"No."

"He hasn't got a summer place, just that one apartment."

"Yes."

"So where?"

Hawes thought for a moment. "How about the cars?" he said.

"What do you mean?"

"The cars. The Caddy and the Buick."

"You mean maybe he's got the stuff in the trunk, or the glove compartment? Something like that?"

"Why not?"

"It doesn't sound like Kramer," Carella said, shaking his head. "I get the impression he was neat, careful. I don't think he'd leave important stuff in the trunk of a car."

"It's worth a try, isn't it?"

Carella sighed heavily. "Anything's worth a goddamn try," he said. "Let's hit the garage."

George's Service Center in Isola was located three blocks away from the late Sy Kramer's apartment. It was there that Kramer had had his cars serviced. It was also there that he had boarded them. George was a wiry little man with grease on his face.

"Let's see your badges," was the first thing he said.

Carella and Hawes showed their shields.

"Now we can talk," George said.

"We want to look over Kramer's cars," Hawes said.

"You got a search warrant?"

"No."

"Go get one."

"Let's be reasonable," Carella said.

"Let's," George answered. "Is it illegal to conduct a search without a search warrant?"

"Technically, yes," Carella said. "But it won't take us—"

"Is it illegal to be doing thirty miles an hour in a twenty-five-mile-per-hour zone?" George asked.

"Technically, yes," Carella said.

"Technically or otherwise, would you call it speeding?"

"I suppose so."

"All right. I got stopped in a speed trap the other day. I've never sped in my life. I'm a careful driver. I was doing thirty miles an hour. Technically, I was speeding. The cop who stopped me gave me a ticket. I asked him to be reasonable. He was reasonable, all right. He gave me a ticket. You want to search those cars, go home and get a warrant. Otherwise, it's an illegal search. I'm being as reasonable as your pal was."

"A speeding ticket makes you a cop hater, huh?" Carella said.

"If you want to put it that way."

"I hope nobody ever tries to hold up your gas station," Carella answered. "Come on, Cotton. Let's get the warrant."

"Good day, gents," George said, smiling.

His revenge had been sweet. It delayed a murder investigation by almost four hours.

They came back with the warrant at four in the afternoon on Monday, July fifteenth. George looked at the paper, nodded, and said, "The cars are inside. They're both unlocked. The keys are in the dashes in case you want to open the trunks or the glove compartments."

"Thanks," Carella said. "You've been very helpful."

"One hand washes the other," George said. "Tell that to your traffic cops."

"Do you know what impeding the progress of an investigation is?"

"All I know is you had to have a warrant," George said. He shrugged. "If you're in such a hurry, now that you got your warrant why don't you go look at the damn cars?"

"We will," Carella said.

Together, he and Hawes went into the garage. The Caddy and the Buick were parked side by side. The Caddy was white, the Buick black. Together, they looked like an ad for good Scotch. Carella took the Caddy, and Hawes took the Buick. They searched the interiors of the cars with patient scrutiny. They removed the seats and looked under them. They felt along the material covering the roofs of the cars, in the hope that Kramer had inserted something between the cloth and the metal. They lifted the floor pads. They took everything out of the glove compartments and everything out of the trunks. The search of both cars took three quarters of an hour.

They found nothing.

"Well, that's that," Carella said.

"Mmm," Hawes said disgustedly.

"At least I've been inside a Caddy," Carella said. "That's the closest I'll ever get to owning one." He studied the white convertible. "Look at that baby, will you?"

"It's a beauty," Hawes agreed.

"And it's got power," Carella said. "Have you ever seen the engine on a Caddy? It looks as if it could power a destroyer. Here, take a look at it."

He went to the front of the car, unclasped the hood, and raised it. Hawes went over to where he was standing.

"It's something, all right," he said.

"Kept it clean, too," Carella said. "A neat guy, Kramer."

"Yeah."

Carella was closing the hood when Hawes said, "Hold it. What's that?"

"Huh?"

"There."

"Where?"

"Stuck to the engine block."

"What?"

"Lift that hood all the way up, Steve."

Carella raised the hood, and then looked at the engine. "Oh," he said, "that's his extra key. It's just a little magnetized box you stick somewhere on the car. An extra key fits into it. In case you lock yourself out of the car by accident."

"Oh," Hawes said, disappointed.

"Sure." Carella reached for the commercially marketed device. "See? The key fits right into this little—" He stopped. "Cotton," he said softly.

"What is it?"

"That's no car key," Carella said. "Holy God, cross your fingers!"

The key stuck to the engine of Kramer's Cadillac convertible had the round, unmistakable yellow, numbered top of a key to a railroad-station locker. There were two big railroad stations in the city, several smaller ones, and several subway stops in which there were pay lockers. It was not necessary to visit each location in an attempt to match the key with the correct locker. Carella put in a call to the company supplying the lockers to the various spots. He gave them the number of the key on the phone, and the locker was pinpointed within five minutes. Within the half hour, Carella and Hawes were standing in front of the locker.

"Suppose there's nothing in it?" Hawes said.

"Suppose the roof of the station caves in right this minute?" Carella said.

"It's possible," Hawes answered.

"Bite your tongue," Carella said, and he inserted the key into the locker and twisted it.

There was a suitcase in the locker.

"Old clothes," Hawes said.

"Cotton, my friend," Carella said, "do not joke. Seriously, my friend, do not joke. I am a very high-strung nervous-type fellow."

"A bomb, then," Hawes said.

Carella pulled the suitcase out of the locker.

"Is it locked?"

"No."

"Well, open it."

"I'm trying to," Carella said. "My damn hands are shaking."

Patiently Hawes waited while Carella unclasped the bag. There were four big manila envelopes in it. The first envelope contained a dozen photostated copies of the letter to Schlesser from the lawyer of the man who'd drunk the mousy sarsaparilla.

"Exhibit A," Carella said.

"Tells us nothing we don't already know," Hawes answered. "Open the next envelope."

The second envelope contained two pages from the ledger of a firm called Ederle and Cranshaw, Inc. Both pages were signed by a C.P.A. named Anthony Knowles. A comparison of the ledger pages showed that the second page was a revision of the first page, and that the first page did not exactly balance. It did not exactly balance to the tune of $30,744.29. The second page balanced very neatly, thank you. Mr. Knowles, whoever he was, had robbed the firm of Ederle and Cranshaw of thirty grand, and then balanced the books to cover the deficit. Sy Kramer had, in his own mysterious way, managed to get a copy of both the original entry and the fraudulent one—and had been using both to extort money from Knowles, who was undoubtedly the $1,100-a-month mark.

"Larceny rears its ugly head," Carella said.

"The skeleton in every closet," Hawes said.

"We'll have to pick up this Knowles."

"Damn right, we'll have to," Hawes said. "He may be the one who done in our friend Kramer."

But, of course, they had not yet opened the remaining two envelopes.

Envelope number three contained six negatives and prints of Lucy Mencken in an attitude close to nudity. Hawes and Carella studied them with something unlike mere professional interest.

"Nice," Hawes said.

"Yes," Carella answered.

"You're a married man," Hawes reminded him.

"She's a married woman," Carella said, grinning. "That makes us even."

"Do you think she killed Kramer?"

"I don't know," Carella said. "But that last envelope better have a lot of answers." He lifted it out of the suitcase. "I think it's empty," he said, with astonishment.

"What? You haven't opened it. How can you—?"

"It feels so light," Carella said.

"Open it, will you? For God's sake!"

Carella opened the envelope.

There was a sheet of onion-skin paper in the envelope, and that was all. The sheet of paper carried a very faint typewritten carbon impression of three words.

The three words were:

I SAW YOU!

Chapter 17

You can carry deduction only so far.

You can add two and two, and get four. And then you can subtract two from four, and get two. You can square two, and get four again. And then you can take the square root of four, and get two again—and you're right back where you started.

There comes a time when your personal mathematics don't mean a damn.

There comes a time, for example, like immediately after the arrest of Anthony Knowles. There comes a time when Knowles admits to the theft and the fraudulent entry in the ledger, and then comes up with a perfect alibi for the night Sy Kramer was killed.

There comes a time when you're right back where you started, and no matter how you add the facts you always get the same answer, and the same answer is no damn good at all.

When that time comes, you play a hunch.

If you're a cop who isn't particularly intuitive, you're up the creek without a paddle. Because then you can only add up the facts, and the facts come out like this:

Kramer was extorting money from three known victims in various amounts, the amounts arbitrarily decided by Kramer in an attempt to make the punishment fit the crime. Three hundred bucks for putting out sarsaparilla that had flavor and body—the body of a mouse. Five hundred bucks for getting undressed—before a photographer. Eleven hundred bucks for making an erasure—to cover a theft.

Kramer had had another source of income. This unknown source had furnished his apartment, bought his cars and clothes, and filled his bank account with $45,000. The first three manila envelopes in the suitcase had dealt with Kramer's low-income marks. The fourth envelope contained a note saying "I SAW YOU!" and this was the car-

bon of a note that had possibly been mailed to someone.
Was the fourth envelope the clue to the big-money mark? If
so, to whom had the note been mailed? And what had Kramer seen?

Facts, facts, more facts.

A man named Phil Kettering had vanished. *Poof,* into
thin air. Why? Where was he now? Had he killed Kramer?
Was he the man to whom Kramer had sent the "I SAW
YOU!" note? And what, what, what the hell had Kramer
seen?

Facts.

Add them up.

Two and two make four.

Or sometimes zero.

Cotton Hawes played a hunch.

He played the hunch on his own time, on one of his off
duty days. If he was wrong, he didn't want to waste the
city's time and money. If he was right, there was plenty of
time to act. And even if he *was* right, there would still be
unanswered questions. He was beginning to wish he'd
signed re-enlistment papers when the war had ended. He
was beginning to wish he was on the deck of a seagoing tug
somewhere in the Pacific, where there was no guesswork,
no suspects, no bodies.

On Wednesday morning, July seventeenth, Hawes
hopped into his automobile. He did not tell anyone on the
squad where he was going. He had made a fool of himself
once before, when he'd first joined the Squad, and he did
not wish to compound the felony by proving himself wrong
another time.

Hawes crossed the River Harb. He drove on the Greentree Highway. He passed the town in which he and an anthropology student named Polly had enjoyed an evening together. The memory was sweet. He drove past Castleview
Prison's impenetrable, forbidding walls. He drove up into
New York State, and he headed for the Adirondacks and
Kukabonga Lodge.

Jerry Fielding recognized the car as Hawes pulled up. He
came down the steps to greet him, his hand extended.

"Been hoping you'd come back," he said. "Have any
luck with Kettering yet?"

"No," Hawes said, taking Fielding's hand. "We can't find
him."

"That looks bad for him, doesn't it?"

"It looks very bad for him," Hawes said. "Do you know these woods pretty well?"

"Like the back of my hand."

"Want to guide me through them?"

"Going to do a little hunting?" Fielding asked.

"In a sense, yes," Hawes said. He went to the car and took out a small travel case.

"What's in that?"

"A pair of swimming trunks," Hawes said. "Could you take me around the edge of the lake first?"

"Are you hot?" Fielding asked, puzzled.

"Maybe," Hawes said. "And maybe I'm cold. We'll know in a little while, I guess."

Fielding nodded. "Let me get my pipe," he said.

It took them an hour to find the spot. The spot was close to the road and close to the lake. The new summer growth had already come in, but it was possible to see the faint traces of deep tire tracks beneath the vegetation. Hawes went to the edge of the lake and looked down into the water.

"Anything down there?" Fielding asked.

"A car," Hawes said. He was already unbuttoning his shirt and trousers. He changed into his trunks and stood poised on the edge of the lake for a moment.

"This is a pretty deep spot," Fielding said.

"It would have to be," Hawes answered, and he plunged into the water. The lake closed around him. The water was very cold for July. The animal and insect sounds of the woods were suddenly cut off. He was in a silent, murky world as he dove closer to the bottom of the lake. The automobile rested on the lake bottom like the hulk of a sunken ship. Hawes seized the door handle and pulled himself to the floor of the lake. Standing erect, clinging to the handle, he tried to see into the car. It was impossible. The lake bottom was too dark. He was beginning to feel the need for air. He pushed himself off and started for the surface again.

When he came up, Fielding was waiting for him.

"Anything?"

Hawes waited while he caught his breath. "What kind of a car did Phil Kettering drive?" he asked.

"A Plymouth, I think," Fielding said.

"The car down there's a Plymouth," Hawes said. "I can't

see into it. We'll need an underwater light and maybe a
crowbar to pry open the doors, if they're locked. Do you
swim, Fielding?"

"Like a shark."

"Good." Hawes came out of the water. "How many
phones do you have?"

"Two. Why?"

"While you're phoning for the gear, I'd like to call the
city. I want to get a positive identification on that car. You
can start with your calls, if you will. I have to go down and
take a look at the license plate."

"If you can't see into the car, how you going to read a license plate?" Fielding asked.

"That's a good question," Hawes said. He nodded.
"Okay, let's get our light."

It occurred to Hawes while they were making the call to
Griffins that they could use a lot more than a light and a
crowbar. And so he ordered skin-diving equipment, complete with face masks and oxygen tanks. The equipment did
not arrive until late that afternoon. He and Fielding went
down to the lake again, equipped themselves, and went into
the water.

Again there was the silence. Again the waters closed
around the diving figures, shutting out the sounds of the
real world. Hawes held the light, and Fielding held the
crowbar. As they dove, Hawes kept thinking, *If this is Kettering's car, if this is Kettering's car* . . .

And then a new thought came to him.

If this was indeed Kettering's car, his hunch would have
been a solid one. The hunch had been simple. He had assumed that Kettering had been killed up here at Kukabonga, which was why they could find no trace of him in the
city. He had never returned from the Adirondacks. He had
been killed here by someone, and his body had been dis-
posed of. The second half of the hunch was equally simple.
Sy Kramer had witnessed the killing, hence the "I SAW
YOU!" note. And the murderer of Phil Kettering was the
person who had been paying Kramer exorbitant sums of
money to protect himself—and this person had had strong
motivation for the second murder, the murder of Kramer
himself.

The new thought that came to Hawes was somewhat
frightening.

For if Kettering had been killed at Kukabonga, and if his murderer was also the man who'd murdered Kramer, what would stop him from killing a third time?

And had not Jerry Fielding been present at Kukabonga when Phil Kettering was killed? And did not Jerry Fielding now hold a crowbar in his hands, and were both men not diving toward the bottom of a dark lake?

If the car was Phil Kettering's, *if* Kettering had been killed, couldn't Jerry Fielding—as well as any of the other men who'd been present—have killed him?

Was Hawes in the water with a murderer?

The idea chilled him. There was nothing to do but wait. He swam toward the rear end of the car. Fielding swam close behind him, the crowbar in his hands. Hawes flashed the light at the license plate. The number was 39X-1412. He repeated it silently several times, burning it into his memory. Then he motioned for Fielding to come to the door of the car. Fielding swam closer. His face behind the mask looked grotesque, evil. He did not seem to be the mild, gently speaking man Hawes had known on the surface. The crowbar in his hands seemed like a deadly weapon. Hawes flashed the light into the car. He could see nothing. He realized, though, that if Kettering were in the car, his body could be on the floor and not visible from the window. He signaled to Fielding again.

Fielding did not seem to understand. He stood motionless, the crowbar in his hands. Hawes swam around the car, trying each door. They were all locked. Then he came back around and pointed to the door near the driver's seat.

Fielding understood and nodded. Together, they applied the crowbar into the space where door met frame. Together they tugged. Together, they pried open the door. Hawes went into the automobile. It occurred to him while he was in the car that Fielding need only slam the door shut on him, wedging it into place again. He would die inside the car as soon as his oxygen ran out. Fielding stood just outside the door now, waiting.

Hawes flashed the light over the floor, before the front seat and the back seat. The car was empty. He backed out of it, and signaled Fielding to the trunk.

Together, they attacked the lock with the crowbar, and then forced open the trunk.

The trunk was empty.

Even if this was Kettering's car, the body of Phil Ketter-ing was not in it.

Together, Hawes and Fielding surfaced.

Hawes wondered if he owed Fielding an apology. He said nothing. Instead, he went back to the house and called the Bureau of Motor Vehicles. They returned his call ten minutes later, telling him that the vehicle bearing the li-cense number 39X-1412 was registered to a man named Philip Kettering who made his residence in Sand's Spit.

Hawes thanked them and hung up. He was not a man to keep things hidden. He would need Fielding's further help, and he wanted to know where he stood at once.

"Don't get sore at me," he said.

"You think I did it?" Fielding asked.

"I don't know. Kettering's car is at the bottom of the lake, and we can't find Kettering or his body. My hunch is that it's buried someplace in those woods, somewhere near where the car entered the lake. My hunch is that somebody at this lodge killed Kettering and was seen by Kramer. Kra-mer began his extortion and signed his own death warrant. Those are my hunches."

"And I was here when Kettering got it—*if* he got it. Right?"

"Right."

"It's your job," Fielding said. "I understand."

"Okay. Where were you on the morning Kettering went into those woods alone—the morning he allegedly left the lodge?"

"I was here until all the men had had their breakfast," Fielding answered. "Then I drove into Griffins."

"What for?"

"Groceries."

"Will they remember your being there?"

"I was there all morning, stocking up. I'm sure they'll re-member. If they don't, they can check the carbon of their bill. It'll tell them what date I made the purchases. I always go into Griffins in the morning. If they've got a copy of the bill, they'll know I was there that morning, all morning. I couldn't possibly have had the time to kill Kettering, shove his car into the lake and then bury him."

"Will you make the call?" Hawes asked.

"I'll dial it. You can talk to the proprietor. His name's Pete Canby. Just tell him what it's all about."

"What date did Kettering leave here?" Hawes asked.

"It was a Wednesday morning," Fielding said. "Let me check my records."

When he came back from his office, he said, "September fifth. I'll call Pete, and you can talk to him."

Fielding called the grocery store, and Hawes talked to the owner. Canby looked up his bills. Jerry Fielding had indeed been in Griffins all morning on the morning of September fifth. Hawes hung up.

"I'm sorry," he said.

"It's okay," Fielding said. "It's your job. A man's got to do his job. Shall we go look for that grave now?"

They looked hard, but they did not find a grave.

Cotton Hawes drove back to the city with another idea, an idea that would almost cost his life.

His murderer was one of three men, that much he knew. Frank Ruther, Joaquim Miller, or John Murphy.

He did not know which one nor, with Kramer dead and Kettering's body probably irretrievably buried in the Adirondack wilds, was he likely to find out which one unless he tried a gamble. He was basing his gamble on Lucy Mencken's reactions to the fake extortionist Torr. Torr had called her with nothing but a threat, and Lucy Mencken had been willing to do business, accepting the lie that someone else had taken over from Kramer.

Hawes hoped the murderer would react in much the same way that Lucy Mencken had reached. If his gamble worked, he would have his man. If it didn't, he had lost nothing and he'd find another way to pinpoint him—he hoped. He made several mistakes in reasoning, however, and those mistakes were what almost cost him his life. One of the mistakes was not letting the rest of the squad in on his plan.

He did not get back to the city until four in the morning. He checked in at the Parker Hotel in midtown Isola, using the false name of David Gorman. From the hotel, and using the phone in the hotel room, he sent three identical wires. One wire went to Ruther, one to Miller, and one to Murphy. The wires read:

I KNOW ABOUT KETTERING. AM READY TO TALK BUSINESS. COME TO PARKER HOTEL, ISOLA, ROOM 1612, AT TWELVE NOON TODAY. I WILL BE THERE. COME ALONE.

                                          DAVID GORMAN

The wires went out at 4:13 A.M. At 4:30 A.M., in all fairness to Hawes, he did call the squad on the off-chance that Carella might be catching. He was not. Meyer Meyer answered the phone.

"Eighty-seventh Squad," he said. "Detective Meyer."

"Meyer, this is Cotton. Steve around?"

"No," Meyer said. "He's home. What's up?"

"Will he be coming in this morning?"

"Eight o'clock, I think. Want me to give him a message?"

"Tell him to call me at the Parker Hotel as soon as he gets in, will you?"

"Sure," Meyer said. "What's the broad's name?"

"I'm in Room 1612," Hawes said.

"I'll tell him."

"Thanks," Hawes said, and he hung up.

There was nothing to do now but wait.

In his mind, Hawes stacked up the attributes of the three suspects. None was an expert shot, but you didn't have to be an expert shot to hit a man at eight feet with a hunting rifle. Murphy was possibly the least likely suspect for a man with a deadly aim—but Murphy was an excellent driver, and the man who'd shot Kramer had been driving a car. Each of the suspects could possibly have paid Kramer the huge sum of money he'd received before his death. Ruther had inherited money, which he said he'd piddled away. He could just as easily have paid it to Kramer. Miller was a land speculator who said he'd made a thirty-thousand-dollar profit. He could easily have made more. Murphy was a retired broker with a fine home and money to throw away on every club in sight, not to mention the upkeep of a Porsche kept in racing condition. He, too, could afford to pay Kramer.

They all looked fairly good.

They all had been in the woods on the morning Kettering allegedly left Kukabonga Lodge.

Any one of the three could have killed Kettering and Kramer.

There was nothing to do but wait. Eventually a knock would sound on the door, and Hawes would open it on the murderer. It was only a matter of time. He had set twelve noon as the appointed hour. He looked at his watch now. It was 5:27 A.M. There was lots of time. He took his gun out of his shoulder rig and put it on the table alongside an easy chair. Then he curled up in the chair and fell asleep.

The knock came sooner than he expected.

He came up out of sleep, rubbed his fists into his eyes, and then looked at his watch. It was 9:00 A.M. The room was flooded with sunlight. There were still three hours to go.

"Who is it?" he asked.

"Bellhop," the voice answered.

He went to the door and opened it, leaving his gun on the table.

The door opened on his murderer.

All *three* of them.

Chapter 18

Each of the three men was holding a gun.

"Inside," Ruther said.

"Quick!" Murphy said.

"Don't make a sound," Miller warned.

The expression on Hawes's face was one of complete shock. The men moved into the room swiftly and soundlessly. Miller locked the door. Murphy went to the window and pulled down the shade. Ruther's eyes flicked to Hawes's empty shoulder holster.

"Where's your gun?" he asked.

Hawes gestured to the table with his head.

"Get it, John." Miller said to Murphy. The old man walked to the table and picked up the gun. He tucked it into his waistband.

"We didn't expect you, Mr. Hawes," Ruther said. "We thought there really was a man named David Gorman. Does anyone know—?"

The telephone rang. Hawes hesitated.

"Answer it," Ruther said.

"What shall I say?"

"Does anyone know you're here?" Miller asked.

"No," Hawes lied.

"Then it's probably the desk. Just speak normally. Answer whatever they ask. No nonsense."

Hawes lifted the receiver. "Hello?" he said.

"Cotton? This is Steve," Carella said.

"Yes, this is Room 1612," Hawes answered.

"What?"

"This is Mr. Hawes speaking," he said.

Carella paused for a moment. Hawes could almost feel a mental shrug on the line. Then Carella said, "Okay, this is Room 1612, and this Mr. Hawes speaking. Now, what's the gag?"

"Yes, I did order breakfast," Hawes said. "Not ten minutes ago."

"What?" Carella asked. "Listen, Cotton—"

"I'll repeat the order if you like," Hawes said, "but I don't see why . . . All right, all right. I ordered juice, coffee, and toast. Yes, that was all."

"Is this Cotton Hawes?" Carella asked, completely bewildered.

"Yes."

"Well, what—?"

Hawes covered the mouthpiece. "They want to send up the breakfast I ordered," he said. "Is it all right?"

"No," Ruther said.

"Let them," Murphy suggested. "We don't want them to think anything strange is going on up here."

"He's right, Frank," Miller said.

"All right, tell them to send it up. No tricks."

Hawes uncovered the mouthpiece. "Hello?" he said.

"Cotton," Carella said patiently, "I just got in to the office. I had a stop to make first, so I just got in. Meyer left a message on my desk. He said to call you at the Parker Hotel and—"

"Come right up," Hawes said.

"Huh?"

"Bring it right up. The room is 1612."

"Cotton, have you—?"

"I'll be waiting," Hawes said, and he hung up.

"What did he say?" Ruther asked.

"He said they'd send it right up."

"How soon?"

Quickly Hawes calculated how long it would take a car with its siren blasting to get to the hotel from the squad. "No more than fifteen minutes," he said, and then immediately wished he had made it a half hour. Suppose Carella had not understood him?

"I only expected one of you," Hawes said. He had quickly reasoned that he was safe until after the alleged bellhop arrived with his alleged breakfast. But if the bellhop did not arrive, how long would these men wait? The thing to do was to keep them talking. When a man is talking, he is not conscious of the time.

"We should have figured that," Ruther said. "The 'come alone' in your wires was very puzzling. If you knew about Kettering, you should have known there were three of us. Why, then, the 'come alone' line? We assumed you meant the three of us alone, no cops. We assumed wrong, didn't we?"

"Yes," Hawes said.

"Do you know about Kettering?"

"I know his car is at the bottom of the lake at Kukabonga, and I figure he's buried in the woods someplace. What else is there to know?"

"There's a lot more to know," Miller said.

"Why'd you kill him?" Hawes asked.

"It was an—" Miller started, and Ruther turned to him sharply.

"Shut up, Joaquim!" he warned.

"What difference does it make?" Miller asked. "Are you forgetting why we came here?"

"He's right, Frank," Murphy said. "What difference does it make?" The old man looked ludicrous with one gun in his hand and another tucked into his waistbank. He looked somewhat like the senile marshal of a cleaned-out once-tough Western town.

"Why'd you kill Kettering?" Hawes repeated.

Miller looked to Ruther for permission. Ruther nodded.

"It was an accident," Miller said. "He was shot accidentally."

"Who shot him?"

"We don't know," Miller said. "The three of us were hunting together. We spotted what we thought was a fox, and we all fired simultaneously. The fox turned out to be Kettering. We heard him scream. He was dead when we got to him. We didn't know whose bullet had hit him."

"It wasn't mine," Murphy said flatly.

"You don't know that, John," Ruther said.

"I do know it. I was shooting a .300 Savage, and you were both using twenty-twos. If my shot had hit him, it would have torn a—"

"You don't know, John," Ruther repeated.

"I *do* know, damnit. Kettering was killed by one of those twenty-twos."

"Why didn't you say so at the time?"

"I couldn't think straight. You know that. None of us could."

"What happened?" Hawes asked.

"We were in the middle of the woods with a dead man," Miller said. His upper lip was beaded with perspiration now. Caught in the grip of total recall, his words came haltingly, with difficulty. "The woods were still; there wasn't a sound. We were hardly breathing. Do you remember, Frank? Do you remember how quiet the woods went after Kettering's scream?"

"Yes," Ruther said. "Yes."

"We stood around the body, the three of us, in those silent woods."

And all at once, Hawes was there with them, standing over a man one of them had shot, standing over a dead man, with the woods gone suddenly still, as still as the man at their feet. And he realized, too, that the men were back there in the Adirondacks, playing out a scene they had lived, playing it with fresh emotion, as if it were happening to them for the first time.

"We didn't know what to do," Miller said.

"I wanted to report it to the authorities," Murphy said.

"But how could we do that?" Ruther asked. "He was dead! Goddamnit, you knew he was dead."

"But it was an accident."

"What difference does that make? How many men get hanged because of accidents?"

"We should have reported it."

"We couldn't!" Miller said. "Suppose they didn't believe us? Suppose they thought we shot him purposely?"

"They'd have believed us."

"And even if they did," Ruther said, "what would a scandal have done to my business?"

"And my job," Miller said.

"Our pictures would have been in every tabloid. And there'd always be the doubt, and the knowledge that one of us had killed a man. How could we have lived with that?"

"We should have reported it," Murphy insisted.

"We did the right thing," Miller said. "No one had seen us. There was no one to know."

"It wasn't murder. We should have——"

"He was dead, damnit, dead! Did you want policemen and reporters barging in on your life? Did you want a living hell? Did you want everything you'd worked for ruined because of a goddamn senseless accident? If the man was dead, how were we harming him further? We knew he was single, we knew his only family was a sister he didn't get along with. What else was there to do? Ruin our own lives because of a dead man? Take a chance that the law would be lenient? We did the right thing. We did the only thing. It was the only way."

"I suppose," Murphy said, and perhaps the argument in the woods had ended the same way, ended with the same false logic, the logic of three panic-stricken men faced with a problem that seemed to have but one solution.

"We buried him," Miller said. "And then we released the brake on his car, locked the doors, and rolled it into the lake. We didn't think anyone had seen us. We were sure we were alone in the woods."

"You should have reported it," Hawes said. "At worst, it was second-degree manslaughter, punishable by not more than fifteen years or a fine of one thousand dollars, or both. At best, it was excusable homicide. An accidental shooting. You might have got off scot-free."

"There wasn't time to consult a lawyer, Mr. Hawes," Ruther said. "There was only time for action, and we acted the way we thought best. I don't know what you would have done."

"I'd have reported it," Hawes said.

"Perhaps. Perhaps not. It's easy for you to coldly say you would have reported it. You were not standing there with the rifle in your hand, and the dead man at your feet—the way we were. Decisions are always easy to make from armchairs. We had a decision to make, and we had to make it fast. Have you ever killed a man, Mr. Hawes?"

"No," Hawes said.

"Then don't make statements about what you'd have done or not done. We did what seemed like the only thing to do at the time."

"We thought it was murder, don't you understand?" Miller said.

"I told you we should report it," Murphy said. "I told you. No! You both insisted. Cowards! I shouldn't have listened to cowards! I shouldn't have listened to frightened men!"

"You're in this, so shut up!" Miller snapped. "How could we have known we were being watched?"

"Kramer," Hawes said.

"Yes," Ruther answered. "Kramer, the bastard."

"When did you get his 'I SAW YOU!' note?"

"The day we got back home."

"What then?"

"He followed it with a phone call. We met him in Isola

one day last September. He said he considered us equally guilty of murder. He had seen the shooting, seen the burial, and seen the disposal of Kettering's car. And since he held us equally guilty and since, he said, we were equally guilty in the eyes of the law, he expected equal payments from each of us. He demanded thirty-six thousand dollars—twelve thousand from each of us."

"That explains the buying spree in September. What then?"

"In October he came to us with another demand," Ruther said. "He wanted an additional ten thousand from each of us, thirty thousand in all. He said that would be the last demand he would make. We couldn't raise the money all at once, so he agreed to take it in two payments, one in October and the next in January. We raised twenty-one thousand in October, and we paid the remaining nine thousand in January."

"We should have known," Hawes said. "Every damn deposit in that bankbook was an odd number divisible by three. We should have realized. What about that April deposit? The fifteen-thousand-dollar one?"

"We didn't hear from him all through the winter. We really began to believe his thirty-thousand-dollar demand was the last one," Murphy said. "Then, in April, he called again. He wanted another fifteen thousand. He swore this would be the last payment. We raised the fifteen thousand."

"Was it the last payment?"

"No," Miller said. "If it had been, Kramer would still be alive. He called again in June, the beginning of June. He wanted another fifteen thousand. That was when we decided to kill him."

"He was bleeding us!" Ruther shouted. "I've just begun to get my agency on its feet. I was pouring every damn cent I'd earned into Kramer's bank account!"

"If homicide is ever considered justifiable," Miller said, "the murder of Sy Kramer was justifiable."

Hawes did not comment. "How'd you do it?" he asked.

"Where's that breakfast?" Ruther wanted to know.

"It'll be here. Tell me how you got Kramer."

"We followed him for a month," Murphy said. "We took shifts. We worked out a timetable. We knew exactly where he went at what hours. We knew his life better than he did."

"We had to," Ruther explained. "We were planning to take it from him."

"Then?" Hawes said.

"On the night of June twenty-sixth we bought a .300 Savage."

"Why that gun?"

"First, because we had some silly notion of disfiguring Kramer beyond recognition. Second, because I own a Savage," Murphy said. "We thought if you ever got around to checking guns we owned, you'd eliminate mine and eliminate me as a suspect at the same time."

"Who fired the gun?" Hawes asked.

The men remained silent.

"You were acting in concert," Hawes said. "It doesn't matter."

"The best shot among us fired the gun," Ruther said. "Let's leave it that way."

"Did Murphy drive the car?"

"Yes, of course," Murphy said. "I'm an excellent driver."

"What did the third man do?"

"He was at the back window with an auxiliary rifle. We didn't want to fire from two different guns unless the first shot missed. We wanted it to appear as if one person had done the killing."

"You damn near succeeded," Hawes said.

"We *have* succeeded," Ruther answered.

"Maybe, and maybe not. A lot of people are on this case. Adding another homicide to it isn't going to help your chances any."

"Will it *hurt* them any? First-degree murder is first-degree murder. You can only burn in the electric chair once."

"Where's the breakfast?" Miller asked.

"What did you do with the rifle you used?" Hawes asked back. A good twenty minutes had passed since Carella's call. Facing the possibility that Carella would never arrive, Hawes began sizing up the men in the room.

"We did just what you thought we did," Ruther said. "We disassembled it and buried the parts in separate locations."

"I see," Hawes said. Murphy was obviously the weakest link. He was an old man who couldn't shoot straight, and he was carrying two guns. Hawes noticed for the first time that the only gun in the room that was not carrying a silencer was his own gun, the gun tucked into Murphy's waistband.

"Did you just buy these guns?" Hawes asked.

"They're part of my collection," Murphy said. "We'll bury them, too, after we use them."

"For a guy who's innocent all the way down the line," Hawes lied, "you're sure joining a sucker's game, Murphy."

"You just finished saying we had acted in concert when we killed Kramer," Murphy said. "I'm an old man, mister. Don't try to pull the wool over my eyes."

"You *must* be old," Hawes said.

"Huh? What do you mean?"

"You're covering me with an automatic that has the safety on!"

"What?" Murphy said. His eyes flicked downward only momentarily, but that was all the time Hawes needed. He flung himself across the room at Murphy, his left hand crashing down onto Murphy's right wrist.

He heard the puffing whisper of a silenced gun being triggered as he hit the old man full in the face, knocking him to the floor. He saw the chunk of wood erupt from the floor not six inches from his head. And then Murphy's gun was in his hand, and Hawes threw himself flat on the floor and fired. The gun made hardly any sound at all. The scene was being played with deadly cold ruthlessness, but it was being played in paradoxical whispers. His first shot dropped Ruther. There were two down now, and one to go.

Miller backed off against the door, leveling his pistol.

"Drop it, Miller!" Hawes shouted. "I'm shooting to kill!"

Miller hesitated a moment, and then dropped the gun. Hawes kicked the gun to one side and then whirled on Murphy. The old man was unconscious, incapable of drawing the fourth gun from his waistband.

Frank Ruther, sitting on the floor clutching his bleeding shoulder, shouted, "Why didn't you shoot him, you fool? Why didn't you shoot him?"

And Miller, standing wearily and dejectedly, answered, "I'm a lousy shot. You know that, Frank. I'm a lousy shot."

It was then that the door burst inward.

Steve Carella lowered his leg from the flat-footed kick that had sprung the lock. His service revolver was in his right hand. He looked around the room quickly. Then he shrugged.

"All over?" he asked.

"*Including* the shooting," Hawes said.

"These our birds?"

"Um-huh," Hawes said.

"The Kramer kill?"

"Um-huh."

"Um," Carella said.

"You sure must have broken a lot of traffic regulations getting here," Hawes said. "Boy, what speed!"

"I thought you were nuts when I first spoke to you on the phone," Carella said. "It took me about five minutes to realize you were in trouble. I thought my call had broken in on you and a girl."

"You've got an evil mind."

"Turns out you didn't need me, anyway," Carella said. Again he shrugged.

"If you'd got to the squad at eight, when you were supposed to," Hawes said, "you could have been here in time for the party."

"I had a stop to make first," Carella said. "I went there from my house, and then I went to the squad."

"Where was that?"

"Lucy Mencken's place."

"What for?" Hawes asked suspiciously.

"I gave her half a dozen pictures and negatives. I didn't like the idea of somebody living in fear for the rest of her life."

"Was she appreciative?" Hawes asked.

"We cooked hot rum toddies over the fire the stuff made. It was very cozy."

Hawes raised one eyebrow.

"*Now* who has the evil mind?" Carella asked.

Hawes made a rule of never replying to accusations that were true. He walked to the phone, lifted the receiver, and waited for an operator. When the operator came on, he said, "Frederick 7-8024, please."

Carella was busily handcuffing Miller to Murphy.

All at once, Hawes felt very sleepy. He yawned.

"Don't go to sleep on us, Cotton," Carella said. "There's a lot of work to be done."

Hawes yawned again and then watched Carella as he walked to the window and lifted the shade. Sunlight spilled into the hotel room.

"Eighty-seventh Precinct, Sergeant Murchison," a voice said.

"Dave, this is Cotton. I'm at the Parker Hotel in Isola. I'll need a meat wagon and some . . ."

Murchison listened patiently, taking notes. Across the street from the station house, he could hear the kids playing in Grover Park. He wished he were a park attendant on a day like this. When Hawes finished talking, Murchison cut the connection. He was about to order the ambulance and the uniformed cops Hawes had requested when the lights on the switchboard began blinking again.

Murchison sighed and plugged in his socket.

"Eighty-seventh Precinct," he said, "Sergeant Murchison."

Another day had started.